Crystal Sage Series 2

1 – Exploration
2 – More Mysteries

by
D. E. Weingand

Crystal Saga Series 2
1 – Exploration
2 – More Mysteries
A Crystal Saga Series

ISBN: 979-8-218-03079-7

Published by D. E. Weingand, Florence, Oregon 97439.

Printed in the United States of America.

Front cover photo by D. E. Weingand.

Luanna K. Leisure, Little White Feather
Graphic Artist and Independent Publisher.

To order additional books go to: **http://www.LuLu.com, Amazon.com or Barnesandnoble.com**

Email: weingand@me.com

Exploration
Crystal Saga Series 2
Book 1

Table of Contents

More Mysteries
Crystal Saga Series 2
Book 2
Table of Contents

Setting and Geography

Akura…the planet

Alteria…the land kingdom which succumbed to the Great Quakes. The remaining land portion is governed by a Council of Elders. Alterians have hazel eyes and blonde hair.

Marinea…the kingdom under the sea formed after the Great Quakes divided the land kingdom of Alteria. Marineans have silver hair and eyes and are governed by a king. They have retractable gills in order to live on both land and sea.

Mosshire…a land kingdom in the cold north composed of small pieces of forested and ice-covered land joined by bridges, ruled by Sostor, an ice magic sorcerer. Residents have fair skin, blonde hair and very blue eyes.

Mesarra…a land kingdom in the south composed of a great desert. Residents are from tribes ruled by Sunan, a solar magic mage. Residents have very dark hair, skin and eyes.

*   *   *   *   *

Primus…a verdant kingdom with many greenhouses and well-designed buildings. Ruled by King Forty, the fortieth king in the sequence of rulers.

Aquelle…a kingdom that includes a huge lake that feeds into the ocean. There are many boats and bridges that offer connections to a series of islands. Previously ruled by King Scimitar; now governed through elections, currently by President Regis.

Timbere…a kingdom situated in a large forest with treehouses linked by aerial pathways. Ruled by Queen Flora III, a Super Sister and Twin to Queen Astrid.

*   *   *   *   *

Brimstone…a mountainous kingdom with many caves. Ruled by King Lucas, a wielder of shadow magic.

(Unnamed Kingdom)…an unnamed kingdom serving the kingdom of Brimstone.

Seaside…a kingdom on the sea. Ruled by Queen Astrid, a Super Sister and Twin of Queen Flora III.

.

Cast of Characters
(Arranged by Kingdom)

<u>Marinea</u>

Tamara…Heroine and Queen of Marinea

Trina…Tamara's sister, and Ambassador to Mosshire

Terra…Mother of Tamara and Trina; also a Watcher

Trident…Father of Tamara and Trina; formerly a prince and King of Marinea; Ambassador to Alteria

Trillium…Trident's twin, and Ambassador to Mesarra

Mia…Tamara's personal attendant

Dr. Astarte…a Medical Doctor serving the royal court

Amanda…Tamara's Social Secretary

Dana, Jon, and Borel...Members of the Security Force's Special Task Force

Mimi and Clark…New members of the Security Task Force

Shamous…Elf owner of **Your Every Wish**, a magical store

<u>Alteria</u>

Trident…Father of Tamara and Trina; husband of Terra; formerly a prince and King of Marinea; Ambassador to Alteria

Terra…Mother of Tamara and Trina; wife of Trident; also a Watcher

Tomas…Executive Assistant to Trident

Fern…A realtor from Alteria and friend of Terra

Mosshire

Sostor…a Super Son/Brother/Twin and ice magic sorcerer on Mosshire. Ruler of the kingdom. Has fair skin, blonde hair and very blue eyes like residents of Mosshire

Rolf…Watcher and temporary ruler of Mosshire

Trina…Tamara's sister, and Ambassador to Mosshire

Mesarra

Sunan…a Super Son/Brother/Twin and solar magic mage on Mesarra. Ruler of the kingdom. Has dark hair and eyes like residents of Mesarra

Trillium…Trident's twin, and Ambassador to Mesarra

Delia…Trillium's first hire, the Embassy Manager on Mesarra

Claud…brief Prime Minister of Mesarra

On the other side of Akura. . .

Primus

Forty…King of the kingdom of Primus on the other side of Akura. (Personal name: **Linc**)

Martine…Marinean Ambassador to Primus

Aquelle

Scimitar…former King of the kingdom of Aquelle on the other side of Akura, masqueraded as a rogue Watcher; sidekick of King Lucas

Regis…Prime Minister of Aquelle

Borel…Marinean Ambassador to Aquelle

Anna… tour guide on Aquelle and first Executive Assistant to Borel

Pieter…second Executive Assistant to Borel

Timbere

Flora III…Queen of the kingdom of Timbere. Super Sister and Twin to Queen Astrid

Brooke…Secretary to Queen Flora

Talia…Marinean Ambassador to Timbere

Brimstone

Lucas…King of the kingdom of Brimstone. Wielder of shadow magic.

Scimitar…former King of the kingdom of Aquelle; masqueraded as a rogue Watcher; sidekick of King Lucas

Seaside

Astrid…Queen of the kingdom of Seaside. Super Sister and Twin of Queen Flora III

Kalia…Marinean Ambassador to Seaside.

Margo…Kalia's guide in Seaside.

On another astral plane. . .

The Crystal Castle

Adele and **Jeremy**…the current Super Beings

Elsa…Watcher at the Crystal Castle

Rogere…Watcher at the Crystal Castle

The Super Children

Solange…Tamara's grandmother and a Super Daughter/Sister, advisor to the Crown. Has silver hair and eyes like Marinean residents and wields clear magic. Twin to Savea

Savea…Solange's twin and Super Daughter/Sister, living near undersea volcanos. Has dark hair, skin and eyes unlike Marinean residents

*   *   *   *   *

Sostor…a Super Son/Brother/Twin to Sunan and ice magic sorcerer on Mosshire. Ruler of the kingdom. Has fair skin, blonde hair and very blue eyes like residents of Mosshire. Wields clear magic

Sunan…a Super Son/Brother/Twin to Sostor and solar magic mage on Mesarra. Ruler of the kingdom. Has dark hair and eyes like residents of Mesarra. Wields clear magic.

*   *   *   *   *

Sean Lockette...A Super Son/Brother/Twin to Jon and possessor of both clear and shadow magic. Leader of the Marinea Security Force

Jon...a Super Son/Brother/Twin to Sean. Member of the Marinea Security Force. Wields clear magic.

*   *   *   *   *

Astrid…Queen of the kingdom of Seaside. Super Sister and Twin of Queen Flora III. Wields clear magic

Flora III…Queen of the kingdom of Timbere. Super Sister and Twin to Queen Astrid. Wields clear magic

Crystal Saga Series 2

1- Exploration

D. E. Weingand

Prologue

My name is Sean Lockette. I am the Commander of the Security Force in the undersea kingdom of Marinea. Queen Tamara and I have just been married and are presently enroute to our surprise honeymoon destination—a gift from the Creator Being.

At the conclusion of the wedding festivities, when we had completed our celebratory voyage down the river running through the kingdom, a white tornado appeared and encircled us, taking us on a journey to that special honeymoon destination. It certainly startled everyone who was watching!

Prior to all this excitement, we had been actively involved in establishing diplomatic relations with the three nearby kingdoms: Alteria, Mosshire and Mesarra; and the newly-discovered three kingdoms on the other side of the planet: Primus, which has volcanic challenges; Aquelle, which is primarily aquatic; and Timbere, consisting of large areas of forest joined by aerial pathways. We are not certain that only three kingdoms are there, and will definitely keep looking.

The cosmology that we all knew made no mention of those kingdoms; nor did it mention the existence of Watchers, the beings initially created to supervise the development of Creation. We were surprised when we found out that Tamara's mother is a Watcher.

What we did know from our cosmology is that the Creator Being wanted to share the glories of Creation and made two Super Beings: one female and one male. The Super Beings decided to make Super Children in their image to amuse them, but became fearful that those Children might have too much power—so they split the Children into two: an original and a mirror image of each one. Each Super Child wore a crystal pendant of power: encased in gold for the originals and silver for the mirror images.

The two female Super Children live in the undersea kingdom of Marinea and have helped administer the kingdom. Marinea was formed as a result of earthquakes and tsunamis that caused part of the Alteria mainland to break off and sink beneath the sea. The Super Sisters Solange and Savea used their powers to make sure all residents had gills to be able to live underwater. Solange is Queen Tamara's grandmother and lives in the Palace; Savea resides near the undersea volcanos.

The males have kingdoms on the mainland of Alteria: Sostor rules Mosshire in the cold north and Sunan governs the southern desert kingdom of Mesarra. Their intentions have often been in question. (Crystal Saga Series 1 has a detailed accounting of our prior adventures.)

Tamara's father, the former King Trident, is now the Ambassador to Alteria. Her younger sister, Trina, is Ambassador to Mosshire. Trident's recently discovered twin brother is Ambassador to Mesarra.

On the other side of our planet, three members of our Security Force are Ambassadors to the three newly identified kingdoms: Martine to Primus; Borel to Aquelle; and Talia to Timbere.

Crystals have been central to our story. Tamara was born with a crystal on her stomach; it became active when she reached puberty and has reflected both her emotions and her needs. Other crystals have appeared on her body when those needs arose. When Trina reached puberty, the nails on her hands and feet became crystals. She also found a blue cloak in her closet that morphs into a waist band when danger threatens.

Both girls received retractable gills with the arrival of puberty, so they can breathe whether on land or sea. Their powers are significant and have proved essential to our survival against various attacks.

I have some personal magical skills that I learned at an academy of magic as a young man. However, my wife and her family are far more powerful. We don't really measure our abilities, but I do know that Watchers and Super Beings wield significant powers. Luckily, in Marinea, we work well together as a team.

Now that Tamara and I are wed, we will be exploring how we can improve our teamwork while investigating new challenges in our environment. It will certainly be wonderful to have a loving partner during this exploration. First on our agenda will be finding out where the Creator Being is taking us—and what we will discover when we get there!

Chapter 1
The 'Special Honeymoon'

The white tornado deposited Tamara and Sean on the steps of the Crystal Castle. This was going to be a different experience than Tamara's astral journeys. Their physical bodies were present now, so there would be no walking through walls. And how they would return home was a mystery.

Climbing the steps, they entered the Castle. Standing in the foyer were Rogere and Elsa, the Watchers/Guardians of the Super Beings who lived there. "Congratulations!" exclaimed the Watchers. "Welcome to your special honeymoon destination!"

"To say that we were surprised would be a serious understatement," announced Sean. "We've never ridden a tornado before!"

"The looks on the faces of our wedding guests and citizens ranged from awe to terror!" added Tamara.

"Don't be concerned," explained Elsa. "Terra has soothed their fears. But you might want to decide together what details you are willing to share when you get home!"

"I know you have been here before, Tamara," Rogere teased, "but it will definitely feel different now—and try not to bump into walls!"

"What can you tell us to expect?" asked Sean.

"We will take you upstairs to a suite of rooms that, to our knowledge, have never been entered by anyone before," said Elsa. "That includes the Super Beings and ourselves. The name of the suite is 'Your Every Wish'."

"That's the name of the shop Shamous owns!" exclaimed Tamara. "Is he connected to this gift?"

"It's possible," responded Elsa, "but we don't really know. Shall we go to the suite now?"

Leading the way, Rogere and Elsa climbed to the top floor. Tamara whispered to Sean, "It was so much easier when I didn't have a physical body to weigh me down!"

Instead of turning toward the living quarters of the Super Beings, Rogere continued on down the hall and stopped at a golden door. He inserted a gold key into the lock and stepped back. "I'm not allowed to turn the key," he explained. Elsa handed them a folder, stating, "Here are your instructions for operating the suite. They should be sufficient. If not, you may call for us—but you must exit the suite in order to actually talk with us."

Exchanging hugs, Sean and Tamara watched the couple

walk away. Looking at each other, they held hands and turned the key together. The door swung open...

Three weeks later, Tamara stretched and yawned. Turning to snuggle back under her covers, she saw Sean lying next to her and smiled. But wait! This room looked like her bedroom, but it was so much larger and the bed itself was enormous! Sitting up in bed, she leaned over and kissed Sean to wake him. He opened one eye and pulled her to him. Opening the other eye, he asked, "Where are we?"

"I don't know," she replied. "It looks like my bedroom, but it's much larger." Looking confused, she added, "The last thing I remember is turning the key to open that suite door. What do you remember?"

"The same thing," he answered. Hearing a knock at the door, they checked each other out to see if they were sufficiently dressed to receive company. Deciding that they were, Tamara called, "Enter."

Mia and Terra came in. Mia put a tray of food on a nearby table and Terra walked to the bed. "Welcome home," she said.

"Mother, do you know what has happened? How long we've been gone? Why my room looks so different?" Tamara asked in a worried voice.

"I can help, but only to a point," answered Terra.

3

"What's the last thing you remember?"

"Opening the door to the suite in the Crystal Castle on our wedding night," responded Sean. "How long ago was that?"

"About three weeks," Terra answered. "I believe the Creator Being has been up to some mischief."

"What kind of mischief? Oh, I remember that the name of the suite was 'Your Every Wish'—like Shamous' shop," replied Tamara.

"That elf is a tricky one," commented Terra. "You can try asking him questions, but I doubt that he will give you true information."

"So we don't know what happened in those three weeks," concluded Sean. "Or whether we made wishes, enjoyed ourselves—or even how we got back home!"

"Some honeymoon!" complained Tamara. "Do you know how or why my bedroom has changed?"

"Let me ask you this," prodded Terra. "How do you feel? Relaxed? Anxious? Physically tired or sore?"

"How about 'all of the above'?" muttered Sean.

"Obviously, you aren't in control of yourselves right now. One thing is certain: your memories have been erased," concluded Terra. "I don't know if they will return. But as to your room, the Sisters remodeled it while you were gone. Since there are now two of you, it needed to be much more spacious."

"Well, they definitely did a good job," assessed Sean. "Please thank them for us."

"You can do that yourselves," suggested Terra. "Everyone is waiting for you on the boat."

*   *   *   *   *

As they walked toward the boat, the Commander noticed that there were no new faux plants in evidence. Hearing cheers of welcome from the boat, they waved enthusiastically and went aboard. The entire Defense Team, plus the Ambassadors, greeted them with hugs.

After everyone took their seats, Terra surprisingly took charge of the meeting. "*As soon as I was informed that they would return today,*" she began, "*I asked you all to attend this meeting. I will preside because Sean and Tamara have nothing to report. Please use mental communication.*

"*The reason that they have no intel to share is that their memories have been wiped. Their last memory was of turning the key to their suite in the Crystal Castle.*"

"*How is that possible?*" cried Trina. "*They were supposed to have a special honeymoon, courtesy of the Creator Being!*"

"*And it may well have been,*" replied Terra. "*I have inquired of Rogere and Elsa, who were the last ones to see*

5

them before they entered the suite. The Watcher Council is launching an investigation and I am hopeful that we will learn something soon. But until then, this meeting is intended to bring them up-to-date on what has happened during their absence. Solange and Savea, I would like to save your reports until last, if that's all right with you." They nodded agreement.

Chapter 2
Reports from Ambassadors

"I'll start then," offered Trina. *"My Ambassadorship in Mosshire started off very well. The Embassy building and remodeling went smoothly and Jon found no listening devices installed. Sostor was a perfect gentleman and, at the opening reception, asked me to dance. I accepted, but during the dance I felt dizzy and had to sit down. Sostor cast a healing spell and I recovered. I reported to both Sostor and Jon that I had eaten one piece off a tray that had been borne by a server just prior to the dance. The assumption was that it was tainted and Sostor is investigating.*

"What spooked me the most was that my crystals hadn't warned me; only my blue cloak did—it morphed into the band around my waist. When we returned to my apartment, it remained on my waist. Jon cast a discovery spell and noticed that ordinary objects in the room had a silver glow.

"Sostor then arrived to check on me. Jon put on my glasses to verify that it was really him—it was—but the ordinary objects were actually surveillance devices. Sostor advised us to be on our guard because strange things had been

7

happening in the kingdom and there were hints of a subversive movement. Jon and I wondered if Rolf had any ties to that movement.

"I sent a message to Mother and she came right away. I asked her if there was any possible connection between Rolf and the rogue Watcher. She left to check with the Watcher Council, returned almost immediately, and told us about a rumor that Rolf and the Watcher were not true Watchers and were really brothers."

"I should interrupt and clarify," said Terra. *"That rumor has been disproved. Rolf was a newbie Watcher and has been reassigned."*

"Mother also suggested that perhaps my crystals didn't warn me because I was not personally in danger," continued Trina. *"My cloak was probably on alert because of those surveillance devices. Jon, do you want to add anything?"*

"Yes," he replied. *"Commander, I feel strongly that we should maintain a Security presence in the Mosshire Embassy. I would like to lead such a mission, if that would be acceptable."*

The Commander nodded and said, *"I agree. Your request is approved until further notice."*

Trina and Jon exchanged smiles—and held hands under the table.

Trillium offered to report next. Surveillance devices had been installed as part of the Embassy construction in Mesarra. Delia, the restaurant server that he had interviewed and hired to be his Executive Assistant, had originally proved to be very capable. But after wearing a pair of magic glasses, he had recently noticed that she appeared as an avatar—and he wondered where the real Delia had been taken.

The first batch of completed job applications were covered with spells, presumably designed to influence his judgment and decision-making. The spell caster was skilled, but Trillium was much better. He created a spell that produced a vid screen above the applications showing the face of the spell caster. He hadn't recognized that person, but knew that he would remember.

Invited to a mandatory state dinner scheduled for the next night, he had been seated at Sunan's right. He had looked over the diners, not recognizing that remembered face—until his gaze fell on the man seated at Sunan's left. Turning to the guest on HIS right, he softly asked questions about his target's identity. "I learned that his name was Claud and was the recently-appointed Prime Minister. What's more, he had been close to the rogue Watcher."

Trillium continued that Sunan had leaned toward him and invited him to a private luncheon the next day so he could meet the Prime Minister. "*I accepted and then asked some general questions about the Prime Minister. When I did so, I noticed that Sunan's eyes glazed over—which worried me. When I saw that Claud's attention was on me, I sent a mental message to Terra, requesting her assistance.*"

At that point, Tamara interrupted and reminded the group that she and Terra had already reported on how they and the Sisters had handled Claud. He was no longer in play and his significant magic had been returned to the Creator Being.

"*So you do remember that?*" asked Jon. "*It's everything after entering your honeymoon suite that has been erased?*"

"*That's correct,*" Tamara affirmed. "*Trillium, is Sunan back to normal, or is something still amiss?*"

"*He's his old self, but his memory of that state dinner and the luncheon the next day is gone,*" replied Trillium.

Terra looked worried. She asked the group, "*Do you remember the 'toys' that I brought back from the Watcher Council? One of them was a memory wiper that could also keep a record of what was erased. I wonder if someone has been using that without my knowledge.*"

"*That's very disturbing,*" claimed Solange. "*I suggest that you retrieve it and bring it here so we can examine it.*" Terra nodded and disappeared.

In a few minutes, she was back with the device.

Activating the memory portion, she held it where everyone could see. Clearly, it had indeed been used. The first images were of the inside of the honeymoon suite. Tamara and Sean leaned forward to observe what they couldn't remember. The suite looked lovely…and then the image faded. The next set of images were of the state dinner and luncheon in Mesarra. The final recording showed the Sisters and Tamara 'melting' the Prime Minister into a puddle of magic.

Solange frowned and asked Terra where she had kept this device and who had access to it. Terra replied that it was with the other 'toys' in a bag she had taken to Alteria. Savea suggested that she should move the bag to Marinea and store it in the Commander's workroom. Terra nodded and once again disappeared. In a moment, she returned and handed the bag to the Commander.

Slumping into a chair, she sighed, "*I agree that it will be safer here—but we still don't know who used it.*"

"*I guess I should go next,*" said Trident. "*Alteria is the last kingdom on this side of the planet. I had to tread lightly since I wanted the Embassy to be housed in the property that Terra and I had already purchased—rather than the building the Elders had procured.*

"*It was a struggle to have a staff that had no prior training or knowledge of basic business practices. There were twelve employees and little knowledge of job descriptions or even an organizational chart.*

"When I asked for a volunteer to schedule individual interviews, only one hand went up. I hired Tomas as Executive Assistant on the spot and he has proved to be both competent and trustworthy. I asked him to chair the meeting where everyone would create their own job description. I stressed that all positions would be probationary until a performance review in six months' time.

"Terra was called away to assist Trillium and her presence at my investiture was uncertain. I was so happy to see her pop in for a few minutes at the critical time and share my moment."

Terra added that she and Tamara had to take an astral journey to the Crystal Castle to consult with the Super Beings and Watchers. They discussed whether Rolf and the rogue Watcher were brothers and discovered only uncertainties. Adele and Jeremy explained that they had installed a 'fail safe' mechanism in their children that would pass their magic into the nearest magical being, in case they were erased. However, no one was certain just who the Super Child on the other side of the planet might be. Tamara and Terra decided to return home and find the Sisters.

Tamara added, *"Terra brought Trillium back to*

Mesarra and we asked him whether he could freeze Sunan so his magic couldn't be accessed—and he said he could. We returned to the palace in Mesarra and Trillium shot a blue bolt at Sunan, who froze in place. The Sisters merged into one being and I placed my hand on theirs. We directed a white bolt of lightning at the Prime Minister and he melted into a puddle of magic on the floor—which Terra returned to the Creator Being."

"And now we shift to the other side of the planet," said Martine. *"Before Savea needed to join Solange, Terra and Tamara in Mesarra, Savea responded to my plea from Primus. King Forty was in denial about the volcanic activity. I was already uneasy because of the surveillance devices that I had found and neutralized—only to have them activate again.*

"When Savea arrived, she was covered in ash. She had found new active volcanos spewing lava, with more about to emerge. She recommended an immediate evacuation and I asked her to accompany me to see King Forty, who finally listened to us. He ordered the evacuation and we watched a huge crack form, taking the palace and the Embassy with it. Most of the present capital city was destroyed. Thankfully, Terra had come to move the population to the eastern side of the kingdom. Fortunately, there was no loss of life. Our goal now is to reestablish the capital, the palace and the Embassy

in the new location."

"Aquelle would be up next," advised Borel. *"The seismic activity just described was causing tsunamis within that mainly aquatic kingdom. King Scimitar had been away when this natural upheaval began, but he returned suddenly and tried to use his considerable magic to stabilize the kingdom. He was not successful and disappeared again.*

"The population had strongly supported an electoral process, rather than reestablishment of royal succession. The Prime Minister, Regis, was the winner of that election. There would be a Legislature and several executive positions in addition to the Presidency.

"I had made Anna my Executive Assistant—but after donning my glasses, I learned that she and many of the staff were not real. I placed wards around the Embassy that would prohibit avatars from entering.

"The next morning, I waited in the Embassy for the staff to arrive—and no one entered. I looked out and saw them sitting on the lawn. After I created a thunderstorm to mask my spell removing all avatars, there was only one person left. His name was Pieter and I appointed him my Executive Assistant. We spent the day creating an organizational chart, job descriptions, and advertisements for staff.

"I believe that the basic structure of the Embassy is on

track to becoming functional. Tomorrow I begin interviewing applicants for our new positions."

"And now I'll talk about Timbere," volunteered Talia. "When I awakened on my second day, I had trouble breathing. I found a snake wrapped around my chest; it must have slithered in using an open space under my window. I resolved to cast a spell to seal myself in, allowing only breezes to penetrate. I also used a rare spell to cover my entire tree house from the outside whenever I left. At last, I felt safe.

"Then I took draft advertisements and an organizational chart that I had created to Brooke in the palace for the Queen's approval. Brooke also shared some job descriptions that had already been vetted by the Queen.

"On the third day, as I approached the Embassy, I found a long line of applicants. I invited them in and began the interview process. I was impressed by seven applicants and invited them back for a second interview. I then put on my glasses and found that most of the applicants were avatars. Fortunately, the seven that I preferred were real.

"That afternoon, I returned to the palace and had a confidential interview with the Queen. We shared private information and I think we will have a good working relationship."

"Thank you for the recaps, everyone," approved

Tamara. *"You were all at the wedding, so that is already shared knowledge. Sean and I have apparently had our honeymoon memories wiped clean. Even looking at the recorded memories on Terra's device didn't clarify anything for me."*

"Or for me," added Sean. *"Does anyone have new intel that occurred while we were away?"*

Hearing nothing, Sean sighed and turned to Tamara, *"I'm very uneasy about this three-week gap in our memories. I don't know where to go from here."*

Chapter 3
Understanding Sean Lockette

"Until we have determined how we will move forward," began Solange, *"I'd like to try an experiment, Sean. With your permission, of course."*

"Certainly, Solange," agreed Sean. *"I always trust you."*

"What magic can Tamara do, that is beyond your capabilities?" asked Solange.

"I see where you're going, Sis," commented Savea. *"I'm intrigued."*

"The most obvious to me," he responded, *"are her crystals and their evolution."*

"I would agree," said Solange. *"Since you returned from the Crystal Castle, have you examined your bodies or clothes for any changes?"*

"I have not, but there really hasn't been any time. We came directly to the boat," he explained.

"I have the sense, even without the memories, that our time together in the Castle suite was loving and mutually enjoyable," interrupted Tamara. *"I would assume that I would have noticed any changes. Could that be why our memories are*

gone?"

"*That's the basis for my question, my dear,*" said Solange. "*I'm going to put a cloaking haze around you and Sean for privacy. Please examine each other carefully and let me know when you have finished.*"

*   *   *   *   *

While Tamara and Sean were cloaked, the rest of the group were asking questions of Solange.

"*Why are you going down this path, Mother?*" questioned Trident. "*You must have a suspicion about something. Would you be willing to share your concerns?*"

"*It's just speculation right now,*" admitted Solange, "*but what if the Creator Being wanted to bring parity to the abilities of the newlyweds?*"

"*How could that be done?*" asked Martine.

"*The Creator Being is all-powerful,*" reminded Terra. "*And there are two uncertainties that I can think of immediately:*

- *What did the Creator Being do with the ball of intense magic that I returned when the Prime Minister of Mesarra was vanquished?*

- *What is Sean's true background? He was a foster child and has no memory of his parents.*

"*Wow!*" cried the group. "*Those uncertainties have not*

18

been thought of until now!"

"I've been thinking along those lines myself," admitted Savea. *"Terra, voicing those uncertainties feels right on target!"*

"Thank you," responded Terra. *"However, I don't know how we can get the answers."*

"The first step is the right question," assured Trina. *"The answers will follow."*

At that moment, the cloaking haze dissipated and the newlyweds emerged. Tamara looked at Solange and affirmed, *"You are right. Sean has a crystal of power around his neck—in a gold setting! And under his long-sleeved shirt, there are crystal bands around his wrists."*

Everyone stared at Sean in awe. Savea looked at Tamara and Sean, daring to ask the obvious question, *"How are your memories now?"*

They spoke in unison. *"Perfect."*

Many questions poured out of the group toward the newlyweds. *"Slow down!"* cried Tamara. *"I can't respond to more than one question at a time. Solange, I'd like to start with you, since you provided the cloaking for us."*

"I did so because I had a hunch that your memories were taken for a reason," explained Solange, *"and that reason could have been because something about you changed*

without your knowledge. Obviously, that hunch proved to be correct regarding Sean. Did anything about you change, Tamara?"

"Not that I'm aware of," replied Tamara. *"Sean, did you notice anything different about me?"*

"Not physically," answered Sean. *"But I'll certainly let you know if I detect something."*

Trina pointed out that change can occur mentally or emotionally, as well as physically.

Nodding, Tamara acknowledged that observation, but also recognized that being part of a couple was bound to influence both she and Sean in many ways.

More questions peppered them: *"What was the honeymoon suite like? What else can you share with us? Why weren't the Watchers allowed into the suite?*

"Those are all good questions," approved Sean, *"but surely you don't expect us to share private memories?"*

"Of course not," replied Savea, *"but do you now remember anything about your past, Sean, that you didn't know before? Perhaps about your life before foster care?"*

"Curiously, I don't," he admitted. *"I had just reached puberty when I found myself in foster care."*

Solange probed further, *"Do you realize that your pendant of power, being encased in gold, signifies that you are the older Super Child after the division?"*

Sean blanched, *"Are you telling me that I am now a Super Child? If so, where did that power come from? Who and where is my other half?"*

"I believe so," admitted Solange, *"From what we now know, the Super Beings created two Children, subsequently divided, on our side of the planet—and one on the other side. They were interrupted from starting another child by the antics of the rogue Watcher in the presentation of the Game."*

"Now my head is starting to hurt!" complained Terra. *"I understand where you acquired that trait, Tamara! I need to go to Watcher Headquarters and see what I can find out."*…and she disappeared.

"What if…" began Savea. *"What if that unnamed rogue Watcher was NOT a Watcher? That possibility has surfaced before. What if he was your other half, Sean? What if he didn't want any competition on that side of the planet and devised the Game to distract the Super Beings from making any further Children? What if he managed to avoid being erased by the Creator Being? What if the Creator Being recognized what was happening and decided to funnel that ball of magic into YOU, Sean, so that your other half could not reclaim it? That would make you a seriously powerful magical being, containing both clear and shadow magic."*

"*Wow!*" exclaimed Sean. "*That's a lot of 'what ifs', Savea. How would we go about verifying any of it?*"

"*I'm hoping Terra will return with some insights,*" sighed Savea.

Minutes later, Terra was once again on the boat. "*I heard your litany of 'what ifs', Savea,*" she asserted. "*You are amazingly on target! By the way, you do know your other half's name, Sean: it's Scimitar*!

Chapter 4
When 'What ifs' = Facts

Tamara and Sean decided to walk slowly from the boat toward the Palace. They were surprised to see the Super Brothers coming toward them. Looking at Sean, Tamara whispered, "*I forgot to invite them to the wedding!*"

Sean squeezed her hand and said, "*Just tell them we decided to keep the guest list within our kingdom.*"

Smiling, Tamara extended her hands to the Brothers and welcomed them to the kingdom.

"*We heard a rumor that congratulations are in order,*" said Sostor. "*Is it true that you two are married?*" added Sunan.

"*Yes, it's true,*" confirmed Tamara. "*We had a simple ceremony attended by friends and family from within our kingdom.*"

"*What other rumors have you heard?*" pressed Sean.

The Brothers looked at each other, shrugged and Sunan offered, shifting to mental communication, "*There's a new rumor that the rogue Watcher may not have been erased from history. Have you encountered that rumor?*"

"*That possibility was just suggested as a 'what if'*

today," admitted Sean. *"Do you believe it could be true?"*

"He was very powerful," affirmed Sunan. *"I wouldn't dismiss it."*

"But how could it be done?" asked Tamara. *"Surely, the Creator Being is more powerful."*

"Of course," Sunan said, *"But the Creator Being doesn't deal in shadow magic…and Scimitar has a high level of command of the shadow forces. It's the only way he could control us."*

"You're scaring me," admitted Tamara. *"How can we combat what we don't understand?"*

"I don't know," shrugged Sunan. *"But I think it may take all of us working together."*

Shifting into host mode, Sean suggested that if the Brothers would like to join them for lunch, they should enter the Palace and go to the Private Dining Room. Nodding, they moved together into the Palace.

*   *   *   *   *

After lunch, the conversation about the fate of the rogue Watcher resumed. *"Since we are reasonably confident that he was not a true Watcher, let's refer to him by his actual name: Scimitar,"* suggested Tamara.

Sean began, *"After the Super Beings confirmed that they had made another Super Child on the other side of the planet, we floated a theory that Rolf and the rogue Watcher (as we called him then) could be those Super Brothers. That theory was eventually debunked, as Rolf didn't seem to have sufficient power."*

"*Did you consider that his Brother could have taken it from him, like Sunan did with me?"* asked Sostor.

"*We did,*" admitted Tamara, "*but that theory was also eventually dismissed.*"

"*Did you ever wonder why only one Super Child was created at that time?*" inquired Sostor.

"*Yes,*" replied Tamara, "*but the Super Beings confessed that their attention was distracted by the Game—which had been provided to them by a Watcher!*"

"*So, if I'm following this correctly,*" analyzed Sunan, "*it would appear that Scimitar was truly half of a Super Child. What was not known was the identity of the other half?*"

Hoping to divert the conversation, Sean asked, "*Sunan, at that State Dinner you hosted, tell us what you remember about your new Prime Minister.*"

"*Sadly, nothing,*" Sunan admitted. "*I have no recollection at all of that evening. I may have had too much to drink.*"

"*And the luncheon the following day?*" asked Tamara. "*What do you remember about that?*"

25

Frowning, he said, *"Again, nothing. I don't even remember being there."*

"Have you ever seen him again?" asked Tamara.

"I never saw him before the State Dinner and I haven't seen him since," recalled Sunan.

"I'm going to ask a hypothetical question," warned Sean. *"If you were Scimitar and you wanted to build a masquerade that you were a talented magical, but not a superstar, how could you mask yourself? Could you temporarily 'park' some of your magic in another magical being?"*

Sunan's face looked puzzled, *"I don't know. That never occurred to me."*

"Pretend that it is possible," pressed Sean. *"If that being with the parked magic were vanquished, could you—or anyone else— reclaim it?"*

"You are spinning some fantastical scenarios, Sean," accused Sostor. *"I'm beginning to think that you know things that should be shared."*

Sean took his memory device from a pocket, pointed it at the Brothers, and fired. The Brothers flinched from the light, and then Sostor asked, "What were we just talking about?"

"Just small talk," smiled Tamara. *"I was asking if you wanted dessert."*

"*No thanks,*" responded Sunan. "*I think we'd better get back to our kingdoms. Thank you for lunch.*" And they both disappeared.

"Well," said Tamara, "*Clearly, they have teleporting skills. I didn't realize that you brought your memory device; what a good idea. I'm not ready to trust them just yet.*"

"*Nor am I,*" added Sean.

*   *   *   *   *

Later, in the Commander's office, Sean and Tamara mentally replayed their conversation with the Brothers. Tamara commented, "*I kept watching my bracelets, and they never reacted to anything that was said. My conclusion is that the Brothers were speaking truthfully. I think what you were suggesting was really confusing them.*"

"*It's against my better judgment,*" replied Sean, "*but I have to agree with you. I think they're as much in the dark as we are.*"

"*However, your hypothetical question opened a new stream of thinking for me,*" speculated Tamara. "*Certainly, that puddle of magic that used to be the Prime Minister was physically molded into a ball by Trillium and transported by Terra. I'm going to summon Mother to participate in this discussion.*"

A knock at the door announced Terra's arrival.

Chapter 5
Pursuing the Possible

"Welcome, Mother," smiled Tamara. *"We are reviewing the luncheon conversation we just had with the Brothers."*

"And you have questions?" asked Terra.

"We do," affirmed Tamara. *"When you returned that ball of magic that used to be the so-called Prime Minister of Mesarra, what happened to it?"*

"The Creator Being accepted it," she replied, *"and I don't know what happened to it after that."*

"I have a difficult question to ask, Terra," said Sean. *"Is it possible that it was part of my transformation, which would mean that I now control elements of both clear and shadow magic?"*

Terra looked shocked, then gingerly sat down on the couch. Tamara put an arm around her mother and added, *"Part of our luncheon conversation included indirect speculation about whether Scimitar could have 'parked' some of his magical capabilities in that Prime Minister so that his own skills would not be fully known. If true, I wonder if the belief that when one half of a divided Super Child is terminated, the other half automatically dies is actually accurate."*

"That could also mean that the Super Beings' assertion concerning a 'fail safe' shift of magic into a nearby magical may not be true," concluded Terra. *"Oh my!"*

"On a personal level," continued Sean, *"Would it be possible for Scimitar to reclaim his formerly 'parked' magic from me, if it is within me?"*

"How much of this conversation was known to the Brothers?" asked Terra.

"I used my memory device to clear their memories before they left," informed Sean.

"Thank goodness," Terra sighed. *"I wouldn't want Scimitar to be able to access their memories. We need to talk to the Sisters immediately."*

*   *   *   *   *

Tamara, Terra, and the Sisters had gathered in the Commander's office. Sean had shared a detailed accounting of the luncheon conversation from earlier that day. Everyone looked worried. Terra stood shakily and excused herself after a few minutes. *"I think she's gone to fact-check some of our identified possibilities,"* said Tamara. *"I've never seen her so upset."*

The office was totally quiet while each individual was absorbed in personal thoughts.

Terra returned to a silent office. Looking around, she could feel the angst that was in the air. There was an overall sense of helplessness that she needed to address.

"I've brought our concerns to the attention of the Creator Being," she began. *"I wasn't sure that I would receive any clarity, but I was surprised. Apparently, we have zeroed in on some sensitive areas that were responsible for some prior decisions. One such decision was declaring the other side of Akura off-limits.*

"The underlying rationale was to allow our kingdoms on this side of the planet to work through issues without complicating our efforts with the problems of distant kingdoms. However, once we entered into seeking diplomatic connections, that mandate is no longer in effect."

"I guess that makes sense," admitted Tamara. *"We have certainly been busy defending our kingdom from various attacks."*

"But now that we've moved forward with diplomacy," added the Commander, *"prior restraint no longer applies."*

"Did the identity of the third Super Child come up?" asked Solange.

"It did," said Terra. *"Once I voiced the question, it was like opening a flood gate! In our many discussions here, we produced many possible scenarios; I"m happy to report that*

there is only one true conclusion. Sean, your pendant of power is encased in gold; this means that you were the original Child. Your mirror image does not reside in either Primus or Timbere; he was king of Aquelle.

"*And that reality opens up a host of other questions. The Super Beings admit to only creating one Child at that time; they were interrupted by your twin seizing the idea of the Game and distracting their attention. Meanwhile, you were set adrift and found a comfortable situation within foster care. That's your first and only memory because you weren't born, you were created as an adult. You subsequently took charge of your destiny and the rest, as they say, is history.*"

"*But I didn't have a pendant of power,*" he stressed. "*Why is that?*"

"*Your Super Parents were so absorbed with the Game, they simply forgot,*" replied Terra. "*In your transformation on your honeymoon, the Creator Being corrected that misstep.*"

"*I have to ask,*" inquired Tamara. "*Could this rocky genesis be linked to yet another imbalance between the two twins?*"

"*I wondered that as well,*" admitted Terra, "*and the answer was 'probably'.*"

"*Could your answer be related to that message on the packaging that I unwrapped, saying: 'A small piece of truth*

32

can disrupt an evil intention'?" prodded Tamara.

"I never thought of that," admitted Terra, *"but you may well be right."*

"Then the next logical step would be to put Scimitar and me together to correct the imbalance," pursued the Commander, *"except that we have no idea where—or if—he still lives."*

"What about that ball of magic that you took to the Creator Being?" asked Savea. *"Was it inserted into Sean? Did it contain both clear and shadow magic?"*

"Yes, yes and yes," replied Terra. *"It is expected that correcting the imbalance between these twins will also redistribute that magic. Plus, as you have probably concluded, the rumor that terminating one twin will automatically destroy the other is a myth."*

Solange and Savea looked at each other and sighed, *"That's a relief!"*

"In that case," added the Commander, *"I think we can assume that Scimitar is still alive. Our challenge is to locate him and convince him to agree to correction of the imbalance."*

Turning to Tamara, he murmured, *"I hope he won't fall in love with you the way I did!"*

Tamara blushed and warned, *"Remember that he doesn't have the twin experiences shared by the Sisters and the*

Brothers. *He may like himself just the way he is—and the behavior that we have observed is that of a spoiled child. Don't underestimate him.*

"*Terra,*" she asked, "*Did the Creator Being comment on whether Scimitar could reclaim his magic by force? Has he learned it's within Sean?*"

Terra looked down and replied, "*Yes—and yes. It is possible. There could be a battle coming.*"

Chapter 6
Seeking Scimitar

On the other side of Acura, to the east of the kingdom of Aquelle, Scimitar rested on a lava throne in an unknown kingdom beneath the sea.   Since he traveled using teleportation, he had never seen the need to develop gills in himself or the artificial residents of his kingdom. His focus was always on himself.

Occasionally he wondered where he had come from. He didn't remember being a child or having friends. HIs earliest memory was awakening in this undersea kingdom—and letting his innate ambition carry him forward. Originally, there were no inhabitants in his kingdom, so he learned to make robots and other forms of avatars to populate it. He discovered that he possessed significant magical skills and, through experimentation, explored both clear and shadow magic.

Curious by nature, he explored every kingdom on the planet. The kingdom of Marinea, under the sea like his own kingdom, intrigued him. When he had found Trillium living homeless in the streets of Marinea, he groomed him and enrolled him in the local Academy of Magical Arts. Ultimately, the boy proved to be a disappointment, refusing to obey his wishes.

At one point, the throne in the kingdom of Aquelle became vacant and he maneuvered events until he became the King. That process had proved to be so easy, that he decided to take over all the kingdoms and rule the planet. Until recently, he had encountered little opposition. However, he now faced pushback from the Queen of Marinea and her supporters.

He had 'parked' some of his magic in that ridiculous faux Prime Minister of Mesarra in order to appear less threatening. She had surprised him when she and those other two women had vanquished the Prime Minister and taken his precious magic somewhere that he couldn't access. He felt weakened without his full power and vowed to reclaim his magic. The Brothers that he had controlled once before had taken back their kingdoms; once he had his full power again, he would teach them a lesson. That Queen would regret interfering with his plans!

*   *   *   *   *

Back on Marinea, Tamara and the Defense Team were totally unaware of what Scimitar was plotting or what he had experienced since being created. They knew they were facing a significant challenge, but the underpinnings were completely unknown.

Meeting on the boat for breakfast continued to be a consistent strategy of communication. Today's agenda would focus on Scimitar; they needed to organize all the diverse details they had gathered and design a way forward. The Brothers had been invited to attend.

Savea began the conversation, *"When I became conscious of being alive and having power, I was confused and disoriented. Solange, how did you feel?"*

"The same," replied Solange. *"But I also remember that we were **together**. Up until our falling-out, we had a lot of time to share thoughts and feelings, time to try and understand not only our present, but what we knew of our past."*

Sostor nodded and agreed, *"We, also, were **together**. Sunan and I were assigned to our kingdoms, but not immediately. We had the luxury of time to figure out what had happened to us."*

"It was very confusing to be unable to remember anything before we just popped into existence," added Sunan. *"Since we both have had personal experience with Scimitar, I wonder if he had any support system, however limited."*

Tamara looked pointedly at Sean, who gave permission with a slight nod. Turning back to the Brothers, she said, *"I have repeatedly brought up the issue of trust: giving trust and gaining trust back when it has been lost. Brothers, the trust between us has been repeatedly given and lost. I'm going to go out on a limb and bestow trust upon you once more, knowing that I am taking a risk. I'm doing this because I trust my bracelets; they have never, since your imbalances were removed, indicated that you were anything but truthful."*

Sostor and Sunan stood and knelt before Tamara. *"We thank you and commit ourselves and our honor to your service, Your Majesty."*

Blushing, Tamara smiled and joked that she should have a sword with which to knight them—and a sword appeared in her hand. Laughing, she touched their shoulders with the sword and declared them '*Knights of the Boat Table!*'

While they had reclaimed their seats, Tamara took Sean's hand and looked at the Sisters, as well as the Brothers. *"You all know that we were on a special honeymoon designed by the Creator Being. It was in a special suite in the Crystal Castle. When we emerged, our memories had been erased and we were unable to share any details. Our memories have been restored and we would like to return to some of the questions that were raised during our luncheon the other day."* Turning to Sean, she invited him to chair the meeting.

"Brothers, you stressed that we would need to stand together. I cannot emphasize that enough. The memories that you and the Sisters just shared were very meaningful—and I

assure you that Scimitar experienced nothing like them. He has been alone since becoming self-aware," Sean emphasized.

"*How do I know this?*" he asked. "*Because, on our honeymoon, I was—in a very real sense—reborn. I became self-aware in the foster child system, with no memory of childhood, previous friends, or family. I worked hard to put myself through the Academy of Magic and learn magical skills.*"

Pulling his pendant out from beneath his shirt, he laughed at the stunned faces before him. "*Terra has just been allowed to confirm that Scimitar is my twin. When he became self-aware, he designed the Game and so fascinated the Super Beings that they forgot to complete the process of creating us— or another Child as well.*

"*And so he and I had no opportunity to bond, as you four did. And while you all agreed to have the imbalances removed, he may be far less interested.*"

"*This makes perfect sense,*" cried Sostor.

"*Welcome to our very special club!*" exclaimed Sunan.

"*Something else occurs to me,*" added Solange. "*The unmade child, if the pattern is followed, should be female. We will need to look into that.*"

"*One more observation,*" suggested Savea. "*Sostor and Sunan are rulers on the mainland. Scimitar was also, of*

Aquelle. Now that he is no longer, might he gravitate, as I did, to a volcanic area?"

"*Or could he have started there?*" asked Sunan.

Tamara rubbed her temples. "*More questions and uncertainties; my head is starting to hurt again!*"

Chapter 7
Where is Scimitar?

Tamara's mental trust meter wasn't 100% positive regarding the Brothers, but she was sincere when she offered to give them another chance. The Defense Team had agreed to allow them to attend some breakfast meetings going forward, in order to share their observations about Scimitar.

There were two primary challenges ahead: locating Scimitar and, once found, convincing him to participate in the removal of imbalances that he and Sean presumably shared.

At the next breakfast meeting, Tamara invited ideas from everyone concerning how to locate Scimitar. The Brothers were attending this meeting, and Sostor began, *"Reflecting on my experiences with Scimitar, I would suggest that Sean try to contact him mentally, twin to twin. Scimitar is so powerful that being physically with him in the same space is very hazardous."*

Sunan indicated his approval of that suggestion, adding that he had personally found resistance to Scimitar very difficult, if not impossible.

"How did he get to be that powerful?" asked Tamara.

"*Brothers, you have shared the same space with him, both individually and together, and yet he seemed to have no problem controlling you.*"

"*I brought that question to the Watcher Council,*" said Terra. "*It was their belief it was the combination of clear and shadow magic that was the significant factor. Since we do not either approve of or use shadow magic, we are presently at a disadvantage.*"

"*Sean, have you experienced any connection with Scimitar as his twin?*" asked Solange. "*Any thoughts, fears, or other sensings? Trillium has told us that he could sense Trident before the two of them actually met.*"

"*I know he's out there,*" replied Sean, "*but he's hiding behind a dark cloud—which I assume is related to shadow magic.*"

"*Dana, are you temporarily in charge of the Security Task Force while Jon and Borel are involved in our Ambassador project?*" asked Tamara.

"*I suppose so,*" answered Dana. "*Mimi and Clark have joined the Task Force in the absence of Jon and Borel. You had charged us with discovering how to defeat shadow magic and I'm afraid that we have yet to be successful.*"

"*Well, that's discouraging,*" admitted Tamara. "*Please redouble your efforts. We have to be able to deal with the shadow arts."*

Savea spoke next, *"This may sound impossible, but I believe that **I** have a weird kind of connection with him through a mutual appreciation of volcanos. I sense that he lives near some, as do I. But he is far away—probably on the other side of Akura."*

"That's very interesting," commented Tamara. *"I'd like you and Sean to work together in establishing first contact. But in acknowledgement of his power, I caution you not to do so physically. Please consider using the astral plane so you can escape easily."*

*   *   *   *   *

Sean and Savea remained on the boat after the others had departed. Sean asked, *"How did you and Solange meet and bond once you were self-aware?"*

"We were standing right next to each other," Savea related. *"The knowledge of originally being one, and now two was just there in our consciousness. That was the way it was supposed to happen. In your case, the Super Beings were distracted by Scimitar and you became self-aware on different sides of the planet!*

"Plus, the pattern here was two Super Children—one male and one female before they were divided. That pattern was never completed when the Super Parents were given the

Game. *So I think that a Super female child has yet to be created. We should talk to Adele and Jeremy about it.*

"*Moreover, I've been thinking about this a lot.*" she continued. "*I don't believe the Creator Being makes mistakes. I think he implanted that ball of magic into you for a reason—and that reason is so that you have some shadow magic with which to combat the shadow magic of Scimitar! If I'm right, we need to figure out how to use it effectively.*"

Sean sighed and responded, "*How do we go about doing that?*"

"*I'm not sure,*" admitted Savea. "*Let's call Terra to help us.*"

* * * * *

It wasn't long before Terra appeared on the boat. "*How can I help?*" she asked. Savea shared her thoughts—and her hope that Terra could shed light on how to proceed.

"*I agreed that the Creator Being does not err,*" Terra replied, "*but offering aid is often not forthcoming. We are usually expected to figure things out independently. I do have one suggestion, however.*

"*When I was transporting the ball of magic, a little piece broke off and I put it in my pocket. I'd forgotten about it, but let's see if there's any shadow magic in it.*" Putting her hand in her pocket, she withdrew a shiny shard that gleamed darkly in the sun. Placing it on the table, she asked Sean to pick it up.

When he tried to obey, the shard moved away. *"Ah,"* Terra nodded, *"It definitely is shadow magic. It's reacting to your clear magic, Sean. How did you feel when you approached it?"*

"Ambivalent," he answered. *"Part of me wanted to grab it, but a greater part wanted to throw it into the river."*

"That confirms that you have access to both forms of magic, Sean," stressed Savea, *"and that the clear is far more powerful than the shadow. Now we need to learn how to control the shadow without being affected by it."*

"I have one more contribution to make," Terra offered. *"One 'toy' I hadn't mentioned, because I didn't know how to use them, is this pair of gloves."* Pulling the gloves from another pocket, she handed them to Sean. *"Put them on, Sean, and then try to pick up the shard."*

Sean complied and reached toward the shard. It stayed motionless, but the edges started to sizzle and then melt. Withdrawing his hand, Sean cried, *"It's a defensive 'toy'! I don't feel threatened by it, but it clearly doesn't want me to touch it. I think if I did, it would be destroyed."*

"Sean, I'm going to levitate it," warned Savea, *"and move it toward you. Let's see what happens."*

Savea reached out her hands and the shard rose off the table, heading toward Sean. As it neared him, he instinctively raised his hands, still encased in the gloves, and the shard backed away.

"Your gloves are protective," commented Terra. *"But I don't know how effective they would be against a large amount of shadow magic. That remains to be seen. How did you feel during this experiment?"*

"In control," he replied. *"But I agree that I might feel differently if the amount of shadow magic I was confronting was much greater."*

"Can you feel which type of magic you are drawing upon?" asked Savea.

"It feels good—and powerful," he reported. *"So I assume it is clear magic."*

"Can you feel the shadow within you?" asked Terra.

"Yes," he responded. *"That's the part of me that wanted to grab the shard."*

"Are you able to activate the shadow while suppressing the clear —and vice versa?" inquired Terra.

"I'll try," he said, removing the gloves. Reaching toward the shard, he made it rise and come toward him. Without actually touching it, he stretched it until it was very thin and formed a barrier. He watched Savea send a narrow

beam of power toward the barrier—where it bounced off.

"*Wow!*" he exclaimed. "*I saw Scimitar repulse beams of power from the Brothers just like that on one of my vid screens. He must have been protecting himself with shadow magic.*"

"*How did you feel internally during this exercise?*" asked Terra.

"*Like I could do anything!*" he answered. "*I sense that this is part of the power of shadow magic. It lulls the wielder into an addictive state that is very dangerous. That might be a weakness in Scimitar that we could exploit.*"

"*Did you still feel in control?*" asked Savea, "*Or did you worry that it might overcome you?*"

"*I was in control,*" he assured her. "*The balance of power within me is predominantly clear magic. Plus, I have never succumbed to any type of addiction, thank goodness.*"

The women looked relieved.

Chapter 8
Finding Scimitar

At breakfast the next day, the topic of Scimitar's whereabouts was on everyone's mind. The Brothers and Terra were again in attendance on the boat. Overnight, Sean had decided not to mention that he had some shadow magic within him; Tamara, Terra and Savea agreed with him.

After eating, the discussion focused on how to find Scimitar. Sean asked the Brothers how they communicated with each other over a distance. Sostor and Sunan looked at each other and admitted that it had always come naturally. Solange and Savea agreed, but Solange also mentioned that when they were estranged, she would picture Savea in her mind and then send her a mental message.

Sean frowned and thought a minute. *"If you want to know where your twin is, what do you do?"*

Solange again answered, *"This is all based on when we weren't behaving as twins. If I wanted to find out her location, I would close my eyes and pretend I was sending out a radar scan until I found her. It usually didn't take long."*

"Could you find the Brothers that way as well?" Sean

wondered.

"*No,*" answered Solange, "*I never tried.*"

"*No and Yes,*" answered Savea. "*I seem to have a weird connection with Scimitar because of our affinity for volcanos.*"

"*One more question for the Brothers: Could you tell the difference between your real twin and an avatar?*" asked Sean.

"*We had a lot of practice,*" responded Sostor, "*but little success. And the new generation of avatars that Scimitar is producing are particularly elusive.*"

"*Why all these questions?*" asked Sunan. "*Have you been trying to find Scimitar by yourself?*"

"*Not yet,*" responded Sean. "*I always like to gather intel before experimenting.*"

"*Well, we are all here to support you,*" Sunan offered. "*Why don't you relax and try sending out some feelers?*"

"*I was hoping you would suggest that,*" admitted Sean.

"*I recommend that your first attempt should be solo,*" Sostor said. "*If that doesn't work, then we can try boosting you.*"

Sean relaxed in his chair and closed his eyes. He pictured the face of the Scimitar avatar they had captured. It felt like he was sending beams of low power outward in concentric circles. Sitting up suddenly, he cried, "*I found him! He's in an undersea kingdom offshore from Aquelle. And I think he felt the scan."*

"*Well done, Sean!*" admired Sostor. "*And you hardly used any power at all. How do you know he felt the scan?*"

"*I saw him react by looking around the room,*" explained Sean. "*I withdrew immediately before he could track me.*"

"*What does your military training suggest that you do next?*" asked Solange. "*Scimitar may be at that location now, but how long will he stay?*"

"*Tamara, you have been so successful in eliminating imbalances,*" began Savea, "*What would you recommend we do next?*"

"*Remember that you four have been willing participants,*" cautioned Tamara. "*I question whether Scimitar will be so forthcoming. If my suspicion is correct, we will have to be more covert in approaching him.*"

"*When you cured our imbalances, we were all present in reality,*" stressed Solange. "*When you dealt with the Super Beings, you were on the astral plane, but the Crystal Castle conditions operated in your favor. Do you think you could be successful trying to work solely on the astral plane?*"

"*I don't know,*" admitted Tamara. "*I would be hopeful that my bracelets would compensate, but there is no guarantee. My comfort level tells me that we would form a cohort of Sean,*" the Brothers, Savea, my mother, and me. Brothers, given your negative experiences with Scimitar, would you agree to this proposal?"

Both Brothers blanched and looked nervously at each other. "*I think our reluctance and fear are very apparent,*" responded Sostor. "*However, the magnitude of this situation forces me to agree to participate. Sunan, how do you feel?*"

"*I share your views, Brother,*" Sunan agreed. "*It will be uncomfortable and terrifying, particularly since his magic is so much more powerful than ours. However, we vowed to support you, Tamara. We stand by that oath.*"

"*Mother, do you have anything to add?*" asked Tamara.

"*I anticipated this outcome of the meeting,*" replied Terra. "*I brought with me the flying belt that I brought from Watcher Headquarters. I believe it is intended for Sean to wear. And Sean, remember to wear your new gloves.*"

Sean nodded and patted his pocket. "*For this mission,*" smiled Tamara, "*I think Sean is our wild card.*"

*   *   *   *   *

The next morning, the new cohort gathered in Tamara's bedroom to begin their unique astral journey. Chairs were positioned on either side of the bed so that everyone would be comfortable.

Tamara welcomed them and added a reminder that

every participant was capable of initiating an astral journey—so if anything went awry, there were alternative ways to return home.

"I don't plan on asking Scimitar's permission to solve the imbalances," she explained. *"I intend to hold Sean's hand and walk toward him. If possible, I will then seize Scimitar's hand and begin chanting. Brothers, I ask you to create an isolating bubble around us—and also provide a distraction if one seems to be needed. Savea, as our volcano expert, do whatever you deem necessary.*

"Mother, are you allowed to actively participate in this mission?" inquired Tamara.

Terra nodded and smiled.

Taking their places, they touched Tamara and tried to relax. Sean and Tamara held hands and her bracelets began to glow. As they all lost consciousness, their spirits rose and surged into the sky beyond Marinea. The mission to find Scimitar was underway!

Chapter 9
Scimitar's Kingdom

Scimitar was disturbed. He had felt the touch of another's mind—and then it was suddenly gone. It was strange, how familiar that touch felt: almost as if he was touching himself! As he fidgeted on his throne, he tried to mentally follow that touch, but it had totally vanished!

Puzzled, he tried to search his memories, but no trace of a similar touch could be found. Standing, he began to pace back and forth. HIs mind was fraught with confusion and bewilderment. Ever since that day when he became self-aware, he had wondered how he came into existence. Clearly, he had never been a baby or a child. There were no memories of that.

The first memory he could identify was the day when he looked into a puddle on a street and saw a grown man. After that mysterious day, he learned more and more about magic and power. As his knowledge grew, his ambition kept pace. He was so close to ruling this entire planet—and then he began to feel pushback from the other side of this world. It was not to be tolerated!

*　　*　　*　　*　　*

Tamara and her cohort neared the dark side of Akura. It was night and they could see the orange glow of volcanic activity both on land and under the sea. Savea gestured that they should fly to the other side of Primus, to the location of the new capital. Once there, she mentally reached out to Martine and found him at his new residence.

He was surprised and delighted to see the astral presence of his friends. When Sean opened his mouth to speak, Tamara shook her head and indicated silence. Sean was confused, but complied.

Tamara raised her hand and pointed to the ring on her finger. She directed the ring to allow communication only with the members of her group. Once that order was in place, she began to mentally issue instructions. *"Mother brought this ring from Watcher Headquarters. It restricts communication to designated listeners and I have just activated it. We have to assume that if Sean were to try and communicate, his twin might be able to find him, so I have ordered silence."* Sean nodded in understanding.

"Martine," continued Tamara, *"Have you encountered any undersea activity that could suggest the presence of an unknown kingdom—possibly ruled by Scimitar?"*

Shocked, Martine thought for a few moments and then replied, *"Actually, I have. After you and Savea produced lava tubes to direct eruption output westward into the sea, an undersea island began to form. When we rebuilt our capital toward the east, I detected similar activity off the east coast. Once you had left for Marinea, there seemed to be forceful actions occurring to reshape that emerging island. At first, I thought it was natural activity but, now that you ask, I'm not so sure."*

"*Thank you, Martine,*" complimented Tamara. "*You have provided the exact intel that we have been seeking. I hope that you and King Forty are making progress reconstituting this kingdom.*"

"*We have been quite busy,*" admitted Martine. "*It won't be long until the new palace is completed. Commander, at some point, when events have calmed down a bit, I'd like to run some ideas by you. If you are willing, just nod your head.*"

Sean smiled and complied.

Tamara reminded the group to keep holding hands and indicated that they needed to follow up on Martine's intel. Waving farewell, they rose into the sky and flew toward the east.

*   *   *   *   *

As they reached the coast of Primus, they looked out to sea and could see an orange glow emanating from deep within the depths off both coasts. They landed on the east shore and

Savea decided to take an exploratory swim. She cast a spell to expand her senses as she dove deeper into the ocean. Her increased hearing alerted her to bubbling lava.

Enhanced vision detected a dome off in the distance. She could smell sulphur and ash. When she reached the dome, another spell allowed her to enter.

Once inside, she could see many figures moving about. While they looked real, she doubted that they were. A long distance away, she spied a structure made of lava that looked like it could be a palace. Deciding to rejoin the group, she teleported back to the shore.

Reporting her observations, Savea asked Tamara whether she wanted to proceed with the mission. Tamara looked around the group and the general consensus seemed to be positive. She reminded everyone of their individual roles in the mission and waved them onward across the ocean to the spot identified by Savea as close to the palace.

Since Tamara, as the leader of the astral journey, was present, the entire group was able to enter through the wall of the dome. None of the figures that Savea had reported seemed to see them, which bolstered their confidence. They moved forward and entered the lava building through a side wall.

Savea's initial identification of this building as a palace proved to be correct. They walked down a central hall and into a room that appeared to be a throne room. Sean spied a figure seated on a throne at the far end of the open space and confirmed that it was Scimitar.

Tamara put on her glasses and verified that the figure was real and not an avatar. She held Sean's hand and advanced to stand before the throne. Since there was no indication that they could be seen, she motioned to Sean to climb up with her to where Scimitar was seated. They each grasped one of Scimitar's hands and she began to chant softly. The Brothers provided an isolating bubble around them, as promised.

The golden haze she had experienced on previous occasions began to surround them and they rose into the air. They rotated in place as her chanting increased in volume. Savea and Terra joined in the chanting, while lightning bolts pierced the haze and they were lowered to the ground.

The haze dissipated, the isolating bubble disappeared, and Scimitar looked at them, seemingly seeing them for the first time. "Who are you?" he asked. "Where did you come from?"

"I am Queen Tamara from Marinea," replied Tamara, "and this is your brother, Sean. The two of you were created with an imbalance which I have attempted to correct. How do you feel, Sire?"

"I feel fine," answered Scimitar, "if a bit tired. You say

this man is my brother? How do you know that? I saw him when I visited your kingdom, but he was in a military uniform."

"You not only visited our kingdom, Sire," added Sean, "but you broke into my office, searching for something. What were you looking for?"

"Are you certain?" responded Scimitar. "I don't remember doing that."

Terra reached into her pocket and removed the fragment of dark magic. Holding it toward Scimitar, she asked, "Could it have been this, Sire?"

Scimitar lunged toward her, but was stopped by a barrier produced by Sean. "Give me that!" he cried. "It's part of what was stolen from me!"

Returning the fragment to her pocket, Terra continued, "It was not stolen. You parked it in the newly-appointed Prime Minister of Mesarra so that you would appear less powerful, and therefore less threatening. Once he was vanquished, that magic was returned to the Creator Being for redistribution."

"But it's mine," he screamed. "Give it back to me and tell me where the rest of it is located."

"It no longer belongs to you," affirmed Terra. "The Creator Being has deemed it so."

"I am more powerful than all of you put together," he

continued screaming. "I will destroy you!" and he raised his hands. Sean stepped in front of Terra and created an ice barrier. Scimitar's magic bounced off the barrier and puddled on the floor. Terra scooped it up and disappeared.

"Where did she go?" yelled Scimitar. "What is happening?"

"I believe she has taken another ball of your magic to the Creator Being," guessed Sean. "Brother, your tantrum is your undoing." Looking at Tamara, he added, "I don't believe the imbalance has been corrected. We should go."

She nodded and touched her travel crystal. They awakened in her bedroom, disappointed in the results of their journey.

Chapter 10
What To Do Next

At the next breakfast meeting on the boat, also attended by the Brothers and Terra, the conversation began with an analysis of what they had experienced on the astral journey. They were beset by feelings of frustration and confusion.

Tamara looked searchingly at her mother and asked, *"Do you think it was because we were on the astral plane? It worked in the Crystal Castle, but the rules are totally different there."*

Terra responded, *"I'm not certain, but I think that may be a likely reason. You were on one plane and Scimitar was on another. He certainly didn't behave as if he was affected in any way."*

"So the element of surprise is gone," commented Sean. *"Tamara, when you and the Sisters vanquished the Prime Minister of Mesarra, you had Trillium freeze Sunan so that his magic wouldn't be in play. Could we consider adapting that strategy?"*

"Actually, I was glad that he did that," approved Sunan. *"I now remember being relieved that the Prime Minister*

couldn't siphon magic off of me."

Sostor frowned, *"But when Tamara was resolving our imbalance, would it have been possible if you were frozen?"*

"That's a really good question," pondered Tamara. *"Sunan, how did you feel when you were frozen?"*

"Like I was watching, as a bystander," he replied. *"I was not part of the action."*

"The piece that we are missing is free will," offered Dana. *"My team has been assigned the mission of dealing with shadow magic. Terra, is there a way that shadow magic can be used to compel acquiescence, even if it would not normally be part of the negotiation?"*

"That's a very interesting thought," acknowledged Terra. *"The Watcher Council has been wrestling with the concept of free will. I'll pay them a visit and see where they are with that discussion."* And she vanished.

"Dana, what has your team learned about the uses of shadow magic?" asked Tamara.

"It's a very complex subject," reported Dana. *"Clear magic is quite straightforward. The shadow arts appear to be used when an extra oomph is required."*

"In other words, when clear magic is insufficient to accomplish what is desired?" asked Tamara.

"That's what we believe," affirmed Dana.

"*So, building upon that belief,*" she continued, "*we are seeking acquiescence from Scimitar that would not normally be available to us—and shadow magic could possibly be a strategy to use?*"

"*I can't tell you how to find it or how to use it,*" said Dana, "*but I think it may be possible.*"

And then Terra returned.

"*Mother!*" cried Tamara, "*Thank goodness you're back. My head is starting to hurt again!*"

"*I listened to your conversation,*" admitted Terra, "*and I think you are on to something. The Watcher Council has debated the issue of free will and concluded that it has to be used voluntarily. HOWEVER, as they worked through the issue, the topic of shadow magic arose. Watchers who had encountered shadow magic testified that it had often been used to compel behavior in others.*"

"*Did they say how?*" asked Dana.

"*The best explanation that I heard was that it was through experimentation and practice,*" continued Terra. Handing Sean a small ball, she added meaningfully, "*Here is the magic I scooped up on our journey. "If you toss it into the air and catch it, it will augment your TOTAL magic.*"

Sean stared at her, then nodded. "*Thank you,*" he sighed. "*Dana, are you meeting with your team this morning?*"

Dana nodded and invited the Commander to accompany him to the meeting. The two left the boat, leaving the rest looking after them with questions in their eyes.

*   *   *   *   *

Later that morning, the Sisters and Brothers were strolling in the garden when Tamara approached them. *"That was quite the interesting conversation this morning, don't you agree?"* Tamara questioned.

"We've been chatting about it since Sean and Dana left the boat," admitted Solange. *"We are uncertain about how to proceed with Scimitar. Our joint opinion is that he would never voluntarily agree to engage in removing the imbalance between Sean and himself. We don't think he either understands what an imbalance is, or that he has one."*

"Remember that Sunan and I had a lot of history between us before you presented the idea, Tamara," added Sostor. *"I doubt if Scimitar has even accepted the idea that he has a brother."*

"Then have you come up with any ideas about what to do next?" asked Tamara.

"Is there anything that you haven't shared with us, Tamara?" inquired Sunan. *"I feel like we're missing something."*

Tamara glanced at the Palace and remarked, *"Look,*

Sean and Dana are back." As they approached, she hurried toward them and gave them both a hug. "*Have you learned anything new?*"

"*Yes,*" replied Sean. "*I've decided to spend some time each day working with Dana and his team, trying to understand shadow magic. I've sent a message to Jon to return and help manage the office. I know Trina won't like that, but we need to move forward on this Scimitar mission.*" Kissing Tamara, he turned and left with Dana.

Tamara turned to the Sisters with a puzzled expression. Sostor took his leave to return to Mosshire and meet with Trina. Sunan shrugged and decided to also return to his kingdom. "*Send me a message if you need me to return,*" he suggested, as he teleported away.

"*Scimitar is turning our world upside down—and he isn't even here!*" sighed Tamara, sadly. Solange and Savea linked arms with Tamara and walked toward the Palace.

Chapter 11
Understanding Shadow Magic

Sean and Dana arrived at the place where Mimi and Clark, the two new members of the Security Task Force, were waiting. Dana informed them that he had briefed the Commander on their progress, and that Sean planned to meet with them every day until there was something substantial to report to the entire Defense Team.

Sean added the news that he had asked Jon to return and assist with managing the office so that there would be time to meet with the Task Force. As they digested that piece of information, Sean swore them to silence about what he was about to disclose.

They listened with rapt attention as he described the transformation that he had experienced during his honeymoon. He showed them his wristbands; he told them about the vanquishing of the new Prime Minister of Mesarra and the transport of the resultant magic puddle, shaped into a ball, to the Creator Being. He shared the knowledge that he was a Super Child, twin to Scimitar, the former king of Aquelle. As he noticed their puzzled expressions, he elaborated with the intel they had acquired about the three additional kingdoms on the other side of the planet.

Reminding them once more that this was secret and privileged information, he assured them that he would brief Jon and Borel when he saw them again.

Then he dropped the bombshell and informed them that he had acquired not only substantial clear magic, but also a supply of shadow magic.

The astonishment on their faces was almost comical. Reaching into his pocket, he withdrew the shard of shadow magic that had broken off the ball of magic Terra had taken to the Creator Being. Holding it where it could be seen by all, he said, *"We now have a physical remnant to experiment upon in our effort to understand what this type of magic is capable of. I caution you not to touch it. Tell me your thoughts and ideas and I will carry out your instructions. I have learned how to deal with it so that it will not harm me, as I am carrying some shadow magic within me at this point."*

Soon, he was pummeled with a barrage of questions, some of which he answered and others he deferred until later. *"Let's get to work,"* he said.

*   *   *   *   *

Meanwhile, Tamara and the Sisters had arrived at the Palace. They headed to the Chapel, entered, and locked the door. Tamara sent a mental summons to her mother, who joined them immediately.

"*Mother,*" Tamara began, "*Sean has left with Dana to meet with the Security Task Force. Do you know why?*"

"*I believe that he is sharing his transformation experience with them as a basis for learning about shadow magic,*" she replied. "*I expect that he has sworn them to secrecy. I would like all of you to take my hands and I will share that information with you. I cannot communicate, even mentally, where any possibility exists that it could be overheard.*"

Tamara and the Sisters complied and a silver haze surrounded everyone. When it had dissipated, they had to sit down; the shock was overwhelming.

"*I had no idea about the extent of his transformation,*" murmured Tamara. "*Oh my!*"

"*With your permission, I need to place a spell on you that will silence you if you accidentally begin to share the intel that I have just given you,*" urged Terra. Seeing nods, she began to chant and the silver haze returned briefly, then left. "*I will now visit Trina and brief her; she needs to know.*" And she vanished.

Tamara looked at the Sisters with shocked eyes. "*I guess we have to trust Sean and the Task Force to take the next step."*

*   *   *   *   *

For the next several weeks, the mission to understand the capabilities of shadow magic proceeded. The overriding question of how Scimitar had managed to independently do so hung over the heads of the Task Force. *"Could he have accidentally found a shard like the one we have?"* asked Mimi? *"Or possibly encountered a wielder of dark magic who taught him?"* suggested Clark.

"Those are good questions," approved Sean, *"and we'll keep them in mind. Our mission here, however, is to channel all our energy into understanding what we have before us."*

Dana raised his hand, *"Sir, I'm going to think of something that I want you to know. Can you use that shard to keep me from telling you?"*

"Let's try," agreed Sean. *"I'm going to focus on the shard and ask it to silence you."* As he did so, a black mist arose from the shard and encircled Dana's head, then melted away.

"Now try and tell me," instructed Sean.

Dana opened his mouth and tried to do so, then shook his head. *"I cannot speak it, Sir."*

"That's real progress!" cried Sean happily.

*   *   *   *   *

At breakfast the next morning, Sean and the Task Force joined the group. They reported a significant breakthrough in their efforts, without providing any details, which they considered classified. *"I believe our next encounter with Scimitar will be much different than our last."* he maintained. *"When we produce a plan for that event, we strongly suggest that it be on the reality plane for everyone involved. Our experience tells us that operating from multiple planes of existence is not effective."*

The rest of the Defense Team nodded agreement. An invitation was sent to the Brothers and Terra to join them for breakfast the following day; they needed to begin work on that plan. There was to be no delay.

*   *   *   *   *

On the other side of the planet, Scimitar lounged on his lava throne, wondering what they were up to. Even with his access to shadow magic, he had been unable to break through and understand the mental communication that they were using. Perhaps he would need to visit Marinea again.

Chapter 12
Confession

The next meeting of the Defense Team would be more than important. Terra and the Brothers were in attendance. The Team needed to create a situation that would attract Scimitar to Marinea. The Commander mentioned the time when Scimitar had entered his office, searching for something, and not finding it. That began a lengthy discussion about what it might have been, with no decision reached.

The Commander sat back in his chair and sighed, "*I need to tell you something. I have been working with Dana and his team to learn about shadow magic.*" Noticing the nods around the table, he continued, "*My interest is both scientific and personal.*"

At that point, he confessed the details of his honeymoon transformation experience and the resultant outcome. "*You are all aware that Tamara and the Sisters successfully vanquished the recent Prime Minister of Mesarra into a puddle of magic. Trillium formed the puddle into a ball and Terra transported it to the Creator Being, because it contained both clear and shadow magic, and was too hot for any of us to handle.*

"*It is my belief that, during my process of transformation, the ball was added to my store of magic. My conclusion is both awesome and troubling. My magical temperature is now off the charts—and it is because I have an undetermined amount of shadow magic as well as a greatly increased supply of clear.*

"*Looking back over these events, I am aware that a shard of shadow magic broke off that ball and was recovered by Terra. I'm guessing that the shard may be what Scimitar was seeking.*"

The shock on the faces of everyone told their reaction. No words were necessary.

The silence was broken by Terra. "*Sean, now that you have shared this much, I think you should complete your story.*"

"*The rest of the story is totally incomprehensible to me,*" he responded. "*What I know is that I was a foster child and, when I came of age, I left and built my life. I have no memories prior to that; I never understood why that was so…until my transformation.*

"*I was led to the awareness that I am one-half of a Super Child created by the Super Beings. On this side of the planet, when the Super Beings made Children to amuse them, the Children were immediately divided to reduce their power and they were able to bond. In my case, that apparently didn't happen. When the division was accomplished, I was located here and my twin was on the other side of the planet, creating a mysterious Game to distract the Super Being parents.*

"To this day, he won't accept that he has a twin brother. I had trouble believing it myself. What I now know is that he is remarkably talented and clever, that he somehow taught himself shadow magic, and that he was NOT erased from history—how he managed that, I don't know. Although we are not identical twins, the Super Children on this side of the planet are also not identical. I am now completely convinced that my twin brother is Scimitar!"

A chorus of gasps followed that revelation.

Sostor looked at Sean and said, *"I knew there was something that you needed to tell us. I never dreamed how profound that intel would be. It becomes more critical now that the imbalances must be corrected. How will we lure Scimitar here—as soon and as safely as possible?"*

Sunan frowned at Sostor and added, *"You and I together could not combat him. Does anyone have any ideas about how we might be successful in the future?"*

"The same way we were able to vanquish that so-called Prime Minister. We need to combine forces: two sets of merged Super Children, plus Tamara, Terra, and the power of Sean,"

answered Savea. "*We can do this!*"

Silence descended on the table. After a few minutes, Sean decided to ask a question, "*Sisters, Brothers—how do you communicate with each other? I know you can do it mentally and with great speed. And is there a difference between sending and receiving?*"

Solange responded first, "*Even when Savea and I were not friends, we still were sisters. I could sense her thoughts and feelings. If I wanted to send a message, I would first mentally get her attention and then send it. If she were trying to contact me, I would feel it inside.*"

Savea nodded in agreement. "*Discord could not separate us. Our relationship is very special, even when fragile.*"

Sostor and Sunan looked at each other. Sunan began, "*I always knew what Sostor was up to, what he was thinking. When I wanted to share something with him, I would visualize his face and then mentally 'talk' to him. When I could feel an interior shiver, I knew he was trying to reach me.*"

"*I always sensed Sunan, even when he wasn't near me,*" affirmed Sostor. "*It was as if he lived inside my skin. I never felt apart from him. Why do you ask?*"

"*I was wondering because Scimitar and I were never*

bonded. I thought perhaps I could try again to recontact him as a brother," proposed Sean. *"One more question: Why do you think we were prevented from bonding? Who or what interfered?"*

"That's a very important pair of questions," stressed Terra. *"As we proceed with our discussion, let's keep them always in mind."*

"Let's try an experiment," suggested Tamara. *"Sean, try and relax and see if you can sense Scimitar like you did before, but this time don't break contact."*

"If I may, Sean," Solange interrupted, *"Would you permit me to cast a relaxation spell that might help you?"*

Sean agreed and Solange rubbed his shoulders while a silver haze encircled them. Sean closed his eyes and sank back in his chair. Suddenly, his eyes opened and he stood, saying *"I feel him. I can tell that he senses me, too. He's confused and doesn't know how to interpret what he's experiencing."*

Sostor suggested, *"Tell him who you are and that you are his brother."*

Sunan broke in, *"Can you tell where he is?"*

Sean answered, *"He's in a dark place—probably the kingdom we previously visited. It looks like he's sitting on a throne made of cooled lava. I introduced myself and he shook his head, as if trying to get rid of my voice."*

"*Suggest that you get together so you can talk in person,*" prompted Sunan. "*Ask him to come here.*"

Sean closed his eyes and tried to send that message. He slumped and sighed, "*I tried and he laughed! I failed.*"

Tamara held his hand and murmured, "*No, you didn't, dear. HE failed. We are dealing with more than an uncertainty. This is a puzzle that is extremely challenging—and potentially deadly. We need to make Scimitar our top priority.*

"*Savea, on a prior astral journey, when we tried to correct the imbalance,*" mentioned Tamara, "*you discovered a dome under the sea on the dark side of the planet. Do you agree that what we saw was Scimitar's kingdom? Didn't it have a lava throne?*"

"*Yes, to both questions,*" agreed Savea. "*But remember that our attempt to correct the imbalance was not successful.*

"*Tamara, would you like to take an astral journey with me? I'd like to visit Trillium and Borel. This would just be for gathering intel. We have already determined that correcting the imbalance has to be done on the reality plane.*"

"*May I join you?*" asked Sean.

"*Of course,*" replied Tamara. "*When would you like to leave?*"

"*Would now be too soon?*" answered Savea. "*I have a feeling that time is not on our side.*"

Chapter 13
Confirmation

Savea and Sean joined Tamara in her bedroom. As they were about to begin the astral journey, Sean asked Savea about her skill set—and couldn't she lead the journey herself. Savea paused and then admitted that Tamara was stronger on the astral plane because of her bracelets. Savea's skills were in teleportation on the reality plane.

As they relaxed, Tamara's bracelets began to glow and the three explorers were on their way. The first stop would be Mesarra to see Trillium. Savea had already contacted him to anticipate their arrival. They soon spied sand dunes ahead and their progress slowed. Landing in front of the Embassy building, they saw Trillium waving at them.

Tamara asked Trillium to direct them to a private setting. He led them into a garden behind the Embassy that offered a table and multiple chairs. Tamara activated her special ring from Terra that would confine their mental conversation to just this group.

Savea opened the discussion by asking Trillium to share everything he could remember about his time with Scimitar.

Trillium responded, *"I know that my magical skills are considerable, but I could not compete with Scimitar's. I believe that he was able to overpower me—and the Brothers as well—because of his command of shadow magic. I'm convinced that, if shadow magic were not in the picture, I could have withstood his efforts to dominate me."*

Sean asked, *"Do you have any idea how he acquired the shadow magic that he uses?"*

"He claims to be self-taught," replied Trillium. *"But I highly doubt that. There must have been some external influence at work. After all, one does not just trip over shadow magic in the street."*

"Don't be too sure about that," objected Savea. *"Shadow magic is basically the perversion of clear magic that has been engineered in the shadows by a twisted mind."*

"But whose mind?" asked Tamara. *"What evil beings exist that would be capable of such intentions?"*

"There is another area of our cosmology that was never taught," explained Savea. *"I came across some documents during my away time with the volcanos. They were impervious to the wrath of seismic activity. Essentially, what they described was the need for balance in the universe.*

"In order to have good, there must also be its opposite. Some beings sought power by going down that evil path. I

didn't understand, at the time, what the underlying message was—but I think I do now. I've wondered why the Creator Being originally declared the dark side of the planet off limits. However, if that was the location of these deluded beings, it would make sense."

"I remember that we once asked the question about other possible kingdoms on the dark side of the planet," added Sean. "We never really pursued that discussion, but I think the time to do so is upon us."

"Thank you, Trillium," approved Savea. "I knew your insights would be helpful. We have one more stop on this astral journey: to speak with Borel, our Ambassador to the kingdom of Aquelle, where Scimitar used to be the king."

Savea stood and hugs were exchanged all around. Before leaving, Sean took Trillium aside and shared his personal intel. Trillium looked surprised, and then delighted. He clasped Sean's shoulders in congratulations.

Holding hands, the astral journey continued.

*   *   *   *   *

They flew eastward, over oceans and forests and mountains until the light turned into darkness. Passing over Primus, they looked down and saw that volcanic activity was still occurring. The next, and final, stop was Aquelle—and a talk with Borel.

Borel was waiting for them outside his Embassy. As before, with Trillium, Tamara asked to be led to a secure and private location. Borel took them to a dock where a large boat awaited. After boarding, he steered the boat out from shore, into the middle of the lake.

"*An excellent choice, Borel,*" complimented Tamara. "*Savea requested this journey, and I'm sure she has questions for you.*"

Savea began, "*Borel, we know that your magical skills are many—which was Sean's intent in nominating you for this position. We are trying to increase our knowledge about Scimitar, who used to be king of this kingdom. Have you learned anything in your short time as Ambassador?*"

"*I've become very aware that the residents of this kingdom were unsatisfied with him as king,*" Borel responded. "*Apparently, his behavior was not unlike that of a spoiled child. He did not seem to care about his subjects and often left the kingdom. He was prone to throwing tantrums and screamed at palace employees.*

"*The end result was essentially a revolution in which the royal succession model was replaced by an election. That election was won by the Prime Minister, Regis, who now rules as President.*"

"*Would you say,*" asked Tamara, "*that he lacked what I*

would categorize as parental control? Did he have any mentors or advisors who could model desirable behavior and mores?"

"I never saw any," said Borel, "and Regis didn't mention anyone. In fact, he spoke of Scimitar rarely. The one thing that did strike me is how often he mentioned Scimitar's absences from the kingdom. No one seemed to know where he went. Since I wasn't here during that time, I couldn't use magical tracing to find out."

"Do you think it might have been possible," asked Sean, "for him to have visited one or more as yet unidentified kingdoms on this side of the planet?"

"Of course it could have happened," agreed Borel, "but there is no evidence that it did—or even that such kingdoms exist."

"I know that you are busy with your new Ambassadorial duties," acknowledged Tamara. "I'm sorry that I have to add to your burden, but please investigate any clues that may occur. This is very important. Before we leave, the Commander has some private intel to share with you that may help your efforts."

She asked Savea to move with her to the rear of the boat so that the men could have some privacy. Looking back over her shoulder, she smiled at the look of astonishment on Borel's face.

Turning to Savea, she asked, *"What do you think about asking my bracelets to look for more kingdoms while we're here?"*

Savea grinned, *"My thoughts, exactly!"*

Crystal Saga Series 2

2– *More Mysteries*

D. E. Weingand

Prologue

My name is Trillium, and I am the identical twin brother of Trident. We have only known each other a short time, as I was spirited away as soon as I was born. My mother, Solange, was not aware that she had birthed twins until we were adults.

I was placed in a foster home as an infant. After I was some years older, I ran away and lived on the streets of Marinea—supporting myself by being a talented thief!

One day, a man came up to me and offered to pay my way to study magic at a special school. I took him up on the offer and he became a mentor to me. The Academy of Magic was great—and I was also provided with lodging and meals!

That lasted for several years and I learned a lot about magic. I actually became a magical prodigy! In later years, when I discovered that my mother was a Super Child and my biological father was a Watcher, I understood where my magical prowess came from.

Then my mentor started to make demands that required me to do things I found distasteful and I refused. He accused me of being ungrateful and I fled the school.

He found me when I returned to the streets and gave me to Sunan, who imprisoned me in his dungeon. (Sunan was also under his control.) My former mentor wanted Sunan to exchange me for Trident and facilitate an invasion of Marinea.

I was ultimately rescued by Queen Tamara, but during that process, an avatar took my place occasionally, confusing people around me because they didn't know how or when to trust me..

I eventually learned that my former mentor was supposedly a Watcher named Scimitar and he was trying to take over all the kingdoms on the planet. Once I was totally removed from his influence, I was finally able to meet Trident, my identical twin. I admit to harboring feelings of resentment because my youth was full of poverty and hardship until the mystery man found me—and Trident was a Prince, and then a King, living a life of luxury.

However, my brother and I had long talks and we were able to share stories about ourselves. Part of being able to do this resulted in an awareness that neither of us had any fault related to our pre-puberty years. We were able to work through our emotions and became close friends.

When Queen Tamara (actually my niece) decided to embark on a project of diplomacy, I was asked if I would be interested in being the Ambassador to Mesarra—Sunan's kingdom. That occurred after Sunan had been released from Scimitar's influence, and I accepted.

It feels so good to have a brother and to be part of a warm and loving family. My childhood might have been a difficult one, but the rest of my life looks promising and welcoming. In fact, the Commander of the Marinean Security Force has just appointed me to the Team led by Dana that is studying shadow magic!

I believe that my considerable skills in magic can contribute to making Marinea a better kingdom, and I will strive to be an excellent representative as an Ambassador.

Chapter 1
New Intel

Once airborne, Tamara instructed her bracelets to seek out kingdoms that had not yet been discovered by her. They started to fly eastward and wound up under a dense cover of clouds for quite a long time. Looking downward, they spotted many trees blanketing the ground as far as the eye could see. *"But where is the kingdom?"* she wondered.

Flying closer to the ground, they observed an extensive mountain range with snow-capped mountains. There were caves leading into the mountains and they dropped slowly to the ground. Deciding to enter one of the caves, they walked carefully into the darkened space. Suddenly, soft lights appeared to guide their way.

When they strode deeper into the mountain, they observed many figures moving about. Their skins were extremely pale and Tamara guessed that living underground was a probable cause. Putting on her glasses, Tamara verified that while many of the figures were real, others were avatars.

Savea pointed ahead where the cave widened into a large cavern. As they approached it, the sound of faint drums and chanting could be heard.

Savea started to move toward the sound when Sean halted and warned, "*Stop!*"

Startled, she turned and asked, "*Is something wrong?*"

Nodding, he replied, "*I can understand the chanting— probably because of the shadow magic in me. This is definitely a location practicing the shadow arts…and the way ahead is fraught with danger. We should leave until we understand more about what we might encounter.*"

Holding hands again, Tamara asked her bracelets to find another unknown kingdom. Within minutes, they were airborne once again, this time headed southeast. Crossing over the mountain range, they approached a grassland dotted with small huts. Large animals grazed in the fields and cultivated land lay directly ahead. This appeared to be a farming community.

Putting on her glasses, Tamara saw many real beings working the farm, with robots as overseers. She sighed in dismay. Clearly, avatars held the power in this kingdom. She shared her observations with Sean and Savea and asked their advice.

Savea said, "*I don't see any evidence of a governing structure. There doesn't appear to be a central urban area. Could this be an area that supports another more affluent kingdom?"*

Tamara offered, *"I'll ask my bracelets."* Almost immediately, they were back at the mountain range and the cave. *"Oh dear,"* sighed Tamara. *"I was hoping this wouldn't be the answer to my question."*

Holding hands again, they rose into the air while she instructed her bracelets to go to another unknown kingdom that was independently governed. They were now headed due south once more and arrived at the edge of a large inland sea. A palace stood on the shore of the sea and multiple dwellings were situated behind it. Further away, a significant urban area stretched out toward the south.

Landing next to the palace, they went in the front door and down a central hall. They followed the sound of voices and entered a large room that looked like a throne room. A meeting was being held at the far end of the space and they moved closer so they could hear what was being said.

An unfamiliar language was being spoken, so Tamara asked her bracelets to translate for the group. The topic being discussed was one of tribute: how much would they have to pay to maintain their independence? One voice complained that they were losing too many residents to the sacrificial fires. Surely there had to be a better way. Another voice cried that magic was evil, but what could they do? Yet another voice stressed that they had to figure out how to fight back—after all, their ancestors never had to face the terrors that besiege us today.

A slim lovely woman sat at the head of the table. The crown on her head indicated royalty. "If only we had allies," she proposed, "we wouldn't have to fight alone. But the magic wielders have isolated our kingdoms so that we cannot band together and oppose them. I pray every day for help in our time of need."

Tamara blanched, then spoke, "*I think this is clear evidence that could explain why the Creator Being forbade venturing to this side of the planet—and now is offering us the opportunity to help. I believe that we have proven ourselves worthy of this challenge. What are your thoughts?*"

Sean reminded her that such a momentous decision needed to be presented to their own kingdom and to other kingdoms that might be affected. He suggested that they return home.

Savea nodded and Tamara touched her travel crystal. They were in her bedroom once more.

Sending her mother a message, she crawled into bed and was fast asleep in seconds. Sean joined her and held her close while she slept.

The next morning, Tamara stretched and found Sean

already dressed for the day. He offered to meet with the Defense Team while she prepared herself for the onset of the day. She agreed and promised to hurry. Asking her bracelets for help, she found herself only fifteen minutes behind Sean as he headed for the boat.

When she reached the boat, she was surprised to find that the Brothers, Terra and the six Ambassadors were aboard. Sean whispered to her that he had invited them since today's discussion could involve them. She reminded everyone to use mental communication and to continue to do so at all times.

"Today's agenda will be of interest to everyone," she stressed. *"The decisions made may have lasting effects on multiple kingdoms. Sean, would you please summarize yesterday's astral journey for the group? And Savea, please add comments as you deem appropriate."*

Sean proceeded to describe their conversations with Trillium and Borel. Savea added relevant details until the Team was satisfied with what they heard. It was clear that their understanding of what they would face when confronting Scimitar had been greatly enhanced.

Moving on, Sean dropped the bombshell that they had discovered more new kingdoms on the other side of the planet. This new intel was so unexpected that members of the Team simply stared at Sean during his report.

Sostor was first to ask a question, "*Tamara, you mentioned that our kingdoms might be affected by what we learned. What did you mean by that?*"

Tamara replied, "*Healthy kingdoms interact regularly. That is why I initiated a project of establishing Embassies with the kingdoms that we knew: familiar ones like Mosshire, Mesarra and Alteria; plus the newly found ones of Primus, Aquelle and Timbere.*

"*We only did a flyover of the latest discoveries, but it was clear that there are problems there. One kingdom obviously is involved with shadow magic; another is subservient to the first, with avatars in charge; and finally, the third is independently governed with a Queen at the helm, but pays some kind of tribute to another kingdom in order to remain a sovereign nation. We heard the Queen begging the universe for allies, for help.*

"*My personal opinion is that the Creator Being declared that side of the planet off-limits because of these troubles. It is also my belief that our kingdoms on this side have demonstrated a maturity and capability of providing aid and assistance. It is our decision now whether or not we will accept the challenge, and which of our kingdoms will participate.*"

Chapter 2
Debating the Decision

Sunan stood and started pacing, mentioning that he thought more clearly in motion. He began, "*I appreciate the clarity of your report, but am overwhelmed by the magnitude of what you have shared. Sostor and I have just reclaimed our kingdoms and have challenges of our own to get them up and running effectively. I personally cannot commit resources to the incredible challenge you describe until my own kingdom is stable and secure.*"

"*I understand your point of view, Brother,*" added Sostor, "*but I would like to toss a theory into this discussion. I am hearing a scenario where we are capable and experienced kingdoms and a plea for help has arisen from a kingdom that is less so. What if...that is a false assumption?*

"*We just emerged from conflicts between our kingdoms that were facilitated by avatars that were developed as robots and androids. For some time, we believed that Sunan had created them. BUT, we have subsequently learned that he— and I—fell victim to an external actor. That actor was Scimitar, who was wielding shadow magic.*

7

"Now we hear that there is a kingdom on the other side that practices shadow magic and has avatars. Consider this: What if it was THAT kingdom which served as the external influence affecting all our kingdoms, beginning with Scimitar, who may be controlled himself? In fact, his prolonged and frequent absences as King might have been because he was visiting that other kingdom.

"If this theory has merit, we have all been victimized by a hostile kingdom and it may be to our benefit to ramp up our defenses by aiding that Queen's cause."

Sean shook Sostor's hand, *"That's a brilliant theory! I hadn't thought of that viewpoint at all! We have been assuming that hostile action was within our world view. Now we can expand our thinking and acknowledge threats that are much farther afield.*

"I'm going to draw upon my military experience to make a few suggestions:

- *That Ambassadors Trina, Trillium and Trident return home and discuss what has been said with the rulers of their kingdoms, returning in one week's time to report back.*

- *That Ambassadors Martine, Borel and Talia try to gather intel, but not share what we have learned. We first will need to figure out if those kingdoms are*

8

working with the newly found ones. You will report back in one week as well.

- *That we take another astral journey to gather more intel about those newly-discovered kingdoms.*

- *That we continue to plan for a reality plane encounter with Scimitar. It would be dangerous to put this on a back burner.*

Savea approved, *"Those are good suggestions, Sean. I recommend that we undertake the astral journey tomorrow after breakfast. I still feel nervous and hear a psychic clock ticking!"*

*   *   *   *   *

The next day, Savea and Sean joined Tamara to begin the astral journey. *"Where should we go first?"* Tamara asked, as she reclined on the bed. Since the bed was now larger, all three could lie together in comfort.

Sean recommended that the third kingdom, the one with a Queen, seemed the most approachable. Savea agreed and they all began to relax. Soon, they were flying away from Marinea, leaving daylight behind and heading toward the darkness.

When they reached the palace that was built on the beach hugging that large sea, they landed and entered through a side wall. Not knowing where they might find the Queen, they roamed the halls, starting with ground level. Tamara asked her bracelets to take them to the Queen and they obliged.

Suddenly, they were on a higher floor and just outside an open door. Looking inside, they saw the Queen at a writing desk, composing a message. She was alone.

Tamara instructed her special ring to include the Queen in their astral conversation and coughed to get her attention. The Queen turned and stared at them, "Who are you? How did you get in here?"

Identifying herself and introducing her colleagues, Tamara explained that they were on the astral plane and had come to ask some questions. She also explained how to communicate mentally for security reasons.

Sean added that they had visited her kingdom the previous day and had heard her desperation. Savea commented that they needed more information in order to make any decision to help.

"*I am Queen Astrid and this is the kingdom of Seaside,*" said the Queen. "*I am so happy to meet you and I hope I can present a convincing argument that will prompt your assistance. I have been the Queen for two decades. At the beginning, this kingdom was peaceful and serene; I was very happy here. Then everything changed.*

"*There are two neighboring kingdoms that are closest*

10

to mine. *We learned the hard way that they were practitioners of shadow magic. Our magical capabilities are not great and we have no contact with the shadow arts. When we were attacked, our defenses didn't hold.*

"The kingdom on our border is not self-sufficient. It serves as a supplier to Brimstone, the kingdom using shadow magic. The King of that shadow kingdom is named Lucas and is a very powerful wielder of the shadow arts. From what I've heard, he has been in power for generations.

"Once he turned his evil attention to Seaside, he demanded tribute from us as a condition of our keeping independent sovereignty. We had no choice but to obey."

"What kind of tribute were you required to provide?" asked Tamara.

"Sacrificial victims," responded Astrid tearfully. *"The religion of that kingdom demands regular feeding of their local volcano in order to maintain their shadow magic practices."*

Savea gasped and collapsed into a nearby chair. Tamara blanched and held tightly to Sean's arm. Sean gritted his teeth and asked, *"What do you know about any weaknesses in that kingdom?"*

"I have no personal knowledge," Astrid admitted, *"and I am unaware that anyone in my kingdom practices shadow magic. I have nowhere to turn for relief. Please help us."*

Sean reached in his pocket and pulled out a small vid screen displaying an image of Scimitar. *"Do you recognize this person?"* he asked Astrid.

Her face turned pale. *"Yes,"* she replied. *"He was the emissary that brought the demands from Brimstone. He is an evil man."*

Promising to return once a decision was made, Tamara touched her travel crystal and they were home.

Chapter 3
Asking Dana for Help

Sitting in the Commander's office, Savea and Tamara waited for Dana and his team to arrive. They needed to know if any progress on understanding shadow magic had been made. Sean leaned back in his chair and pondered what they had learned on their astral journey.

A knock on the door indicated that the Security Team had arrived. "Enter," called Sean and waved the team to some available chairs. *"We need to know everything that you have discovered. Marinean defenses have to be strengthened as soon as possible. We are in imminent danger."*

"What has happened, Sir?" asked Dana.

Sean briefly summarized their astral journey and the expressions on the faces of the Team grew increasingly grim.

"Are we going to help that Queen?" asked Dana.

Tamara responded, *"I think this is a situation where we need to be proactive. If we do nothing, the danger will come to us. However, we have huge knowledge gaps. We need to know how to combat a shadow magic assault."*

Savea added, *"And we don't know if any other kingdoms*

will join us. There is a possible scenario in which we are alone in this endeavor."

"I certainly empathize with Queen Astrid," admitted Tamara. *"When I assumed the throne, hostile attacks were frightening—but nothing like what she has been facing. While I don't want to put our kingdom in danger, I am convinced that inaction would be a far worse choice."*

Savea asked if she could invite Solange and Terra to the meeting, and everyone nodded agreement. They immediately appeared in the room, followed by a surprise visit by the Brothers.

Sean welcomed everyone and provided additional chairs. He commented that seeing this unexpected assembly of power was heartening.

Sostor spoke first, *"Sunan and I have had many discussions about what faces us—and we have reached a consensus. Although we recognize that our duty compels us to put our kingdoms first, to do so while putting them also in harm's way would be irresponsible. Therefore, we agree to join in the challenge that you proposed."*

Sean shook the hands of both Brothers and invited them to sit while he brought everyone up-to-date on what they had learned during their last astral journey.

When he began to relate what Queen Astrid had shared,

the horror on the faces of everyone in the room brought Tamara to the brink of tears. She added details to Sean's accounting, emphasizing that what had occurred—and was still happening in the kingdom of Seaside—could be replicated on this side of the planet if they did nothing.

Savea added a plea: *"We must figure out a way to stop the kingdom of Brimstone from continuing and expanding its evil activities before it is too late for all of us. But while we are focused on that, we must keep our attention on Scimitar as well. I don't have a clear idea of how deep his role is in all of this. I'm even beginning to have doubts about whether he is actually your twin brother, Sean. We must keep all intel on the table and examine it carefully."*

"What are you suggesting, Savea?" asked Sean. *"I thought the evidence was clear that he is my twin brother. What has raised doubts in your mind?"*

"I have questions about the timeline," she responded. *"What you have shared about when you became self-aware is much more recent than what Queen Astrid told us about Scimitar's involvement with Brimstone. It just doesn't ring true."*

Tamara had been closely monitoring her bracelets during this discussion and found no evidence that truth was not present. She injected this observation into the conversation and all talk ceased for a few minutes. Solange then posed the obvious question: *"If not Scimitar, then who?"*

"I have no idea," answered Savea. *"I've been wrestling with that notion myself."*

"I think we should leave that issue on the table and move to the report from Dana and his team," proposed Sean. *"What have you learned? What can you tell us?"*

"Since Jon has returned from Mosshire, I've asked him to join us," said Dana. *"He was the original leader of this team and may have some clarifying comments to contribute as we proceed."* Jon had been sitting quietly in the corner, without being noticed. He pulled his chair closer to the group, and thanked them for permitting him to listen to the conversation.

Dana continued, *"We have examined many examples of clear magic as well as what few shadow magic instances that we could locate. There are a lot of similarities between the two types. What is completely different, however, is intent. Clear magic is focused on improving what is occurring. Shadow magic appears to be an add-on, designed to change the present magic into a different and negative force."*

Jon agreed, *"That is what I was observing before I turned the Team over to Dana. While I have been visiting Mosshire, did the Team find any other attributes of shadow magic that are new or different?"*

"*Yes,*" replied Dana. "*Once the Commander gave us a shard of shadow magic to analyze, we discovered that there was a relationship between the two types of magic that is similar to what magnetic devices experience—particularly in terms of spatial relations.*"

"*Commander,*" pressed Jon, "*where did you get a shard of shadow magic?*"

"*From Terra,*" he replied. "*It broke off the ball of magic that was recovered from the recent demise of the new Prime Minister of Mesarra. The Team has been scientifically studying how the two types of magic interact.*"

"*Don't forget about your gloves, Sean,*" reminded Terra. "*Jon, I brought them back from Watcher Headquarters. They seem to affect dark magic spatially.*"

"*In what way?*" asked Jon.

"*The shard retreated when the gloves approached it,*" explained Sean. "*That made us realize that the gloves could be used defensively.*

"*Terra, would it be possible to find out from the Watcher Council whether large amounts of the material from which the gloves were made could be secured?*"

"*That's an interesting and important question,*" she replied. "*I'll check on it immediately.*" And she disappeared. In a few minutes, she returned. "*No one on the Council knows* where the gloves came from," she reported. "*So that's yet another uncertainty that needs to be investigated.*"

Sean sighed, "*The pile of uncertainties continues to expand. Dana, what direction is the Team going to explore next?*"

"*Right now,*" answered Dana, "*that is unclear. But if anyone has any encounter with shadow magic, please inform us. We need to gather all data that becomes available.*"

"*Meanwhile,*" added Jon, "*I am very uncomfortable with our lack of information about shadow magic and the potential danger that it presents. Commander, I would like to rejoin the Team in addition to my duties in the office. I believe that Trina is safe now in Mosshire and we have serious challenges to the kingdom ahead.*"

"*Permission granted,*" said Sean. "*Let's meet on the boat as usual tomorrow morning and continue this discussion.*"

Chapter 4
Decision Time

The next day, after eating breakfast on the boat, the expanded Defense Team began to chart the way forward. A decision needed to be made regarding whether help would be offered to the kingdom of Seaside.

A lively discussion covered the pros and cons of whether help would be given. When all arguments had been exhausted, a vote was taken. It was no surprise to anyone that the potential hazards of no involvement outweighed the significant concerns that had been identified. It was agreed that Tamara, Jon and Savea would undertake an astral journey the next day to bring the news to Queen Astrid.

Tamara took Terra aside and asked, *"Mother, there's a nagging thought in the back of my mind. Would you be willing to visit Trillium in Mesarra and consult with him for me?"*

"Of course, dear," replied Terra. *"What do you want to know?"*

"He told us when he was here that he gets a 'creepy feeling' when he is near the real Scimitar," Tamara answered. *"Yet, when we determined that the Scimitar who came here was*

an avatar, Trillium had that same feeling. Could it be possible that the King of Brimstone has improved his development of avatars so much that they cannot be identified as artificial? I am very concerned that it could be true, and we need to know. It is also possible that shadow magic is involved."

"*I'll visit him right away,*" promised Terra. "*Try not to worry needlessly. I'll be back as soon as I can.*"

*   *   *   *   *

The next day, Tamara, Jon and Savea met in her bedroom to prepare for the astral journey. Terra had not as yet returned from Mesarra, but as they lay on the bed, Terra ran into the room and joined the journey.

As they flew from light into darkness, Terra began to share what she had learned from Trillium. "*Trillium has a lot of experience to share with Dana's team. I recommend that he be appointed immediately.*

"*As to your concerns, he was surprised that the avatar fooled him. But revisiting that memory, he supports your theory that the King of Brimstone, using shadow magic, could fabricate avatars that appear identical to real beings—even to fooling the glasses. If that is the case, then we don't know if Scimitar has ever been real and may have only been an avatar all along. That would certainly explain why your attempt to correct imbalances could not be successful.*"

"*This is very troubling, Mother,*" sighed Tamara. "*What we thought was true has once again been turned upside down. If Scimitar has always been an avatar, there is no way that he is Sean's twin brother. We shall have to reconsider that question as well.*"

Reaching the Seaside kingdom, the four travelers landed and entered the palace. They returned to the room where Tamara had met the Queen on the last journey, but she wasn't there. Tamara asked her bracelets to lead them to her and they complied. Moving down a hall, they found an open door to what looked like a bedroom and saw the Queen sitting on her bed, crying.

Tamara knocked gently and entered the room. The Queen looked up, startled, and then recognized Tamara. "*I hope you have decided to help us,*" she cried, wiping her eyes. Tamara sat next to her and asked why she was crying.

"A new demand for sacrificial victims has just been delivered," she sobbed.

"*What will happen if you don't obey?*" asked Savea, switching to mental communication.

"*An army of avatars will attack my kingdom,*" she replied, as tears rolled down her cheeks.

"*How long do you have to meet the demand?*" asked Jon.

"*Only one week,*" she sobbed. "*I just can't do it, but my kingdom will be destroyed if I don't.*"

"*What can we do?*" Tamara asked the team. "*Would our magic work on the astral plane here?*"

"*I don't see why not,*" assured Terra. "*You and the Sisters vanquished that Prime Minister while on an astral journey.*"

"*Savea, can you construct a defensive dome over this kingdom?*" asked Tamara. "*If so, how long would it take you?*"

"*I can,*" she replied, "*but King Lucas is reported to be a very powerful wielder of shadow magic. He probably could destroy it with ease.*" She asked Queen Astrid, "*How close is his kingdom to the ocean? or to volcanos?*"

Queen Astrid responded, "*The ocean is quite far, but the inland sea is here. And volcanos are everywhere, mostly underwater.*"

"*Tamara,*" asked Savea, "*are you wearing that special ring that your mother gave you?*"

"*Yes, of course,*" replied Tamara.

"*Ask it to restrict communication to just between us for a moment,*" requested Savea.

"*Done,*" said Tamara. "*What do you need?*"

"*There is a massive power surge in this room,*" warned Savea, "*King Lucas will detect it right away. He will investigate with an army at his side. Take us home immediately, and Queen Astrid, too."*

"Everyone touch me," ordered Tamara as she reached for her travel crystal…and they were back in her bedroom.

*   *   *   *   *

"What has just happened?" Jon asked.

"You know that I am a Super Child," began Savea, as she sent a message to Solange to come and bring Sean with her. *"What you may not know is that Super Children can always detect when another one is near. That happened to me in Seaside."* Solange and Sean entered the room just as she made that last statement.

"But Savea," Solange interrupted, *"You were the only Super Child on the journey."*

"That's true," affirmed Savea, *"But I wasn't the only one in Queen Astrid's bedroom. We had to return quickly before King Lucas found us."*

"I'm confused," admitted Tamara. *"Savea, please explain."*

"Tamara," Savea began, *"When you and Sean were on your honeymoon and his transformation started, what were you doing?"*

"I felt compelled to place my hands on his chest," she replied.

"And then what happened?" asked Savea.

"We were surrounded by a golden haze and when it dissipated, there was a pendant of power encased in gold around his neck," Tamara related.

"Just as I suspected," affirmed Savea. *"Tamara, please stand in front of Jon and do the same action."*

Tamara complied. The remembered golden haze appeared and when it vanished, Jon was wearing a pendant of power encased in silver.

"Now do the same action to Queen Astrid," ordered Savea. Tamara did so, and a pendant of power encased in gold appeared around her neck.

"And this is why there was a massive power surge in Astrid's bedroom," explained Savea. *"We had to escape the looming wrath of King Lucas."*

Tamara sank into a chair. *"My head is beginning to hurt again,"* she complained.

Chapter 5
Understandings

Everyone in the room looked stunned. Solange turned to Savea and asked, *"How did you know?"*

Savea replied, *"It was the size of the power surge that convinced me. Jon, what is the first memory that you have?"*

Jon answered, *"I'm not sure. I do remember looking into a puddle and seeing myself as an adult man, around the age of puberty. I spent the next few years exploring Marinea and taking on small jobs to feed and clothe myself. When the Commander appeared and posted job notices, I was intrigued and applied right away."*

Sean walked over to him and clasped his shoulders. *"You became self-aware around the same time that I did. But we didn't recognize each other as brothers—why was that?"*

"You hadn't received your pendants as yet," prompted Savea. *"That was necessary for full awareness."*

"I don't know if any imbalances exist," commented Solange, *"but I don't think it would hurt to try the correction, Tamara."*

Tamara nodded and held the hands of the two men. A

golden haze surrounded them and they rose into the air, turning around in place. When they landed, the now aware Super Brothers hugged each other in delight. *"We have always been close, but this is so special,"* exclaimed Sean. *"Everything feels so right!"*

Tamara smiled and asked Terra, *"I thought the other Super Child was supposed to be on the other side of the planet?"*

"That was the intention," agreed Terra, *"but their creation was incomplete because Scimitar had lured the Super Beings into playing the Game."* She then walked over to Queen Astrid. *"I'm sure that you are confused, my dear. Let me explain to you what has just transpired."* She led Queen Astrid to a quiet corner of the room and held her hands while she spoke.

Returning to the center of the room, Terra told the group that Astrid's Super Sister was still unknown. That uncertainty would have to be resolved—hopefully, soon. What was certain, however, was that the absence of that second Super Child had been corrected. Having the Sisters at the helm of Seaside would definitely be a strong deterrent to King Lucas.

*   *   *   *   *

Before heading back to Alteria, Terra spent a few minutes with Sean. She supported Trillium's wish to be appointed to Dana's team; she could confirm that he had experiences that would prove beneficial. *"Since Jon is now a Super Brother, he has the ability to teleport Trillium. Serving on that team would not negatively affect his diplomatic duties,"* she stressed. *"We need to utilize all the benefits available to us if we are to combat shadow magic effectively."*

Sean nodded his agreement and asked Jon to fetch Trillium and also the other Ambassadors as soon as possible. Moving to Tamara's side, he suggested that the Brothers and the Ambassadors be invited to the next day's breakfast meeting. *"They need to be updated on all the eventful happenings of this amazing day,"* he proposed. Putting his arms around her, he kissed her deeply—not even noticing that they had been left alone by the rest of the group.

*   *   *   *   *

The next morning, everyone gathered on the boat for the usual breakfast. However, since the Ambassadors were present, it turned out to be more of a reunion. As before, Tamara turned the meeting over to Sean for his summary of recent events. Although this was old information for most of the group, the expressions on the faces of the Ambassadors were priceless!

Trina squealed, *"Jon, you're a Super Brother?! How cool is that?!"*

Trident looked stunned. He was trying to absorb the fact that both his daughters were in love with Super Children!

Borel frowned and then asked about the newly-discovered kingdoms. *"Are you satisfied that all the kingdoms have been located now?"*

Tamara responded, *"Everything is still on the table. We have many uncertainties—and few certainties. But we are still working on unravelling the mysteries."*

Talia sat quietly before commenting. When she did, it was a tearful request. *"I have reported that Queen Flora and I shared confidential information. I really like and respect her. I propose that we investigate whether she might be the Super Sister that is currently unidentified. If that were true, I believe it would solve some major issues. Could we somehow pursue that line of inquiry?"*

"Since Tamara was successfully on the plane of reality, we would need to either teleport her to Timbere or bring Queen Flora here," said Sean. *"Which approach do you recommend?"*

"I think it would be less intrusive to do it in Timbere," recommended Talia. *"Queen Tamara, would you be agreeable?"*

"Of course," replied Tamara. *"I would love to meet her, Queen to Queen. I have just had the pleasure of meeting Queen Astrid of the kingdom of Seaside. I suspect that she would also*

be interested in participating in such a mission."

Sean thought for a moment, then addressed his Brother, *"Jon, you have been busy teleporting Ambassadors to this meeting. I think it is my turn to practice my skills. Tamara, I will join you, Queen Astrid and, hopefully, Terra tomorrow following breakfast and we will proceed to Timbere. Jon, I'd like you to take Talia back to Timbere today so she can prepare Queen Flora for our visit."*

"That's a good strategy, Sir," agreed Jon.

Laughing, Sean commented, *"Jon, since we are Brothers, I think we have earned the right to be on a first name basis!"*

Flushing, Jon nodded.

After congratulating the new Super Brothers, Sostor chuckled and added, *"If you two have questions about sibling etiquette, Sunan and I are available to you!"*

After a good general laugh around the table, Tamara asked Savea, *"Before leaving Seaside, you had asked Queen Astrid about the locations of the seas and volcanos. What did you have in mind?"*

"It may—and likely will—be necessary to access both in defense of Seaside. I need exact intel about their whereabouts. And if you and Queen Astrid are agreeable, it would also be helpful to have an Ambassador in place," responded Savea.

"*Your request is important,*" judged Tamara. "*Sean and I will get back to you as soon as possible.*

"*Are there any other comments or questions today?*" Hearing none, Tamara thanked everyone for coming and concluded the meeting.

Chapter 6
The Mission to Timbere

Later that day, Jon took Talia home to Timbere. She sat in her treehouse for a while, considering how she should present tomorrow's visit to Queen Flora. At last, she stood and headed to the palace.

When she arrived, she went to Brooke's office and requested an audience with the Queen. The door to the Queen's office opened and Queen Flora invited her in. "I heard your voice," she explained.

There were several items on Talia's mental agenda. "Your Majesty...

"Please, first names only in this office," reminded Flora.

"Right. Sorry," Talia apologized. "I just returned from Marinea and need to discuss some important issues." She then explained how to proceed using mental communication.

"How did you get there and back so quickly?" asked Flora.

"When I was growing up," replied Talia, *"I learned the cosmology of my kingdom and what was then known of our planet. Do you have a similar cosmology?"*

"*I do not,*" admitted Flora. "*Please share with me what you learned.*"

Talia thought to herself, "*This could take a while*" as she proceeded to do as requested. When she had finished, Flora asked for more details about the Super Beings and Super Children. Once Talia had shared more information, including the division of the Super Children, Flora leaned back in her chair and thought for several minutes.

After waiting in silence, Talia brought up tomorrow's visit. "*A party of three people will join me, hoping that you will allow an audience,*" she proposed. "*I hope that you will. I take full responsibility for this visit.*" She then told Flora about the Seaside kingdom to the east, the identification of the Queen as a Super Child, and the shadow magic kingdom of Brimstone. She followed this news with intel about Scimitar and the possibility that he was an avatar all along, and not real.

At that point, she brought up the subject of the glasses and their failure to identify a superior type of avatar. Flora blanched and gasped, "*You are truly full of good news today!*" she cried.

"*I actually hope that I am bringing good news,*" responded Talia. "*While I was in Marinea, I asked permission to arrange tomorrow's visit, and this is why. I am hoping—and want to verify—that you might be the unknown Sister to Queen*

Astrid of Seaside. If you are willing, tomorrow we will know the answer."

"*Why would I be unknown?*" asked Flora.

"Because Scimitar interrupted the creation by giving a magical Game to the Super Beings, distracting them from completing the process," Talia explained.

"*This all sounds fantastical,*" commented Flora, "*but I will permit the meeting so we can be certain, one way or another. I appreciate your endeavors on my behalf, Talia. I hope your suspicion is correct.*"

"*As do I,*" assured Talia. "*If I may ask, what is your earliest memory?*"

"*That's a curious question,*" replied Flora. "*I have no memories of childhood. My first memory was of looking into a bathtub and seeing the image of an adult woman.*"

"*I'm so happy to hear that!*" cried Talia.

The two women rose and exchanged hugs. Talia went home with hope in her heart.

*   *   *   *   *

At mid-afternoon the next day, Talia welcomed Sean, Tamara, Terra and Queen Astrid into her treehouse. She smiled broadly as she related that Queen Flora would see them and that no knowledge of cosmology was traditional in this kingdom. "*She asked for a briefing on our cosmology and I*

33

was happy go do so. AND I asked about her earliest memory and it was looking into bath water as an adult! I'm so hopeful!"

"It sounds very positive, Talia," assured Tamara. *"I hope your theory is correct. Shall we go the palace and find out?"*

They walked on the aerial pathways leading to the palace. Talia was nervous, but tried to take deep breaths. When they arrived at Brooke's office, she introduced everyone; the door to the Queen's office opened and Flora bid them to enter.

Talia repeated the introductions to the Queen and everyone took a seat. Tamara began by explaining what was about to take place. Queen Flora rose and walked to the middle of the room. Tamara also rose and stood before her, placing her hands on Flora's upper chest. The familiar golden haze arose. When the haze dissipated, a pendant of power encased in silver was around Flora's completely normal neck. Her exo-skeleton dropped to the ground.

"I was RIGHT!" cried Talia. *"You ARE a Super Child! AND you are healed*!!"

Queen Astrid stood and ran to her Sister. They hugged and cried together. Tamara stepped forward and said, *"There's one more step. We don't know if there is an imbalance between you, as there have been with other Super Children, but it won't harm you if we try to correct it. Please hold each other's hands and also mine."*

The golden haze returned and the three women rose into the air, turning in place. After a few minutes, they settled back on the ground and hugged again. There were smiles all around and Flora called, "Brooke, bring some celebratory wine!"

Turning to Talia, Flora kissed her cheeks and hugged her tightly. *"I owe everything to you. What can I do to repay you?"*

"Love and enjoy your Sister, and help her when you can," Talia answered. *"Do a lot of talking, for you have a mutual enemy."*

*   *   *   *   *

Before they left, Savea had instructed Astrid and Flora in how to teleport so that they could remain in contact easily. Astrid decided to stay in Timbere for a few days, so the others would return to Marinea without her.

Terra hugged the newlyweds before rejoining her husband in Alteria. Tamara and Sean asked Talia if she had any time to show them around Timbere. She gladly agreed to do so, and they cheerfully enjoyed the tour.

Privately, Tamara worried that everything was just a little too rosy. Shadow forces were in play; she wondered if they were prepared for what might come—and how soon.

Chapter 7
Evil Never Sleeps

During the time that Queen Astrid had spent in Marinea, Savea used that opportunity to question her about the location of water sources and volcanos near Seaside and Brimstone. Although Astrid's intel lacked detail, there was a significant amount of helpful information. Savea believed that she would be able to find and utilize adequate resources once she was back in Seaside.

The Commander focused time and energy on creating new surveillance birds that were tailored to cruise the newly discovered kingdoms of Brimstone and Seaside. In addition, both he and Jon spent time with Dana's Team, trying to learn more about shadow magic. When he returned to his office, he found Tamara waiting for him.

"Sean, we need to appoint an Ambassador to Seaside," she reminded him. *"Do you have any recommendations?"*

"I've been looking over my Security Force roster and one name has captured my attention. Her name is Kalia. Her skills include long-distance swimming, surfing, and underwater Games. She has adequate magical abilities, but

nothing exceptional. However, she is a quick learner and seems to get along well with everyone. Shall I send for her?" he asked.

Tamara nodded enthusiastically. *"We need to put an Ambassador in place quickly. Please do."*

*   *   *   *   *

After a successful interview, Tamara asked Kalia whether she would be interested. Hearing a positive response, she inquired when she would be able to report to her new posting. Kalia looked at the Commander and asked what would be convenient that wouldn't disrupt the Security Force. They agreed that she could plan on one week.

Tamara then suggested to Kalia that she travel first to Timbere, to spend a few days with Talia, who could provide valuable insight into running an Embassy. Kalia sighed in relief, grateful that she would have an opportunity to ease into the position. Sean promised to notify Talia of Kalia's appointment and arrange for Jon to transport her to Timbere. He was confident that Queen Flora would see to the further transport to Seaside.

Next, Tamara sent a summons to Savea, who appeared a few minutes later. Introducing her to Kalia, Tamara asked Savea to spend some time with Kalia during the next week, as she expected them to be working closely together in the future.

After the Ambassadorship had been settled, only one more duty remained: to notify Queen Astrid that her Ambassador-designate had been appointed and would be assuming the position after spending some time with Talia in Timbere. Tamara intended to take care of that today.

Sinking back into the cushions on the couch in Sean's office, she closed her eyes for just a moment. Sean looked up from his desk, recognized what was happening, and rushed to her side as he observed her bracelets starting to glow. Together they embarked on an unanticipated astral journey.

*   *   *   *   *

Soaring eastward from light into darkness, they eventually saw the snow-covered mountains below. Dropping to the ground in front of a cave where interior lights were glowing, they crept inside and moved silently ahead. They saw a man wearing a crown chastising Scimitar.

"You have to be tougher with that Queen," he yelled. "She can be easily intimidated. We need more sacrificial victims if we are going to increase the amount of shadow magic available to us!"

Scimitar cringed with fear and tried to explain his lack of success. "She won't be alone anymore," he said. "Marinea has authorized a woman to come as an Ambassador to Seaside. But she isn't here yet. I still have time."

"How do you know about this Ambassador?" asked the King.

"You forget that my magic is very strong," boasted Scimitar. "I can even reach into people's dreams."

"And YOU forget that your avatar body keeps you from being one of the sacrificial victims!" the King threatened. "Remember what happened to your former body!"

"How could I forget?" whined Scimitar. "You made me watch my body as it was sacrificed!"

"Stop being such a crybaby!" insisted the King. "If you stop being useful to me, I'll sacrifice you anyway!"

"You weren't always so cruel, Sire," observed Scimitar. "I remember when you practiced only clear magic…before you discovered those ancient volumes in this cave."

"I wasn't powerful then," admitted the King. "I much prefer things the way they are now. Now figure out how to get me those victims!!!"

"*We need to protect Queen Astrid from Scimitar!*" exclaimed Tamara. "*And then come back to look for those ancient volumes.*"

Sean reminded her that Astrid had gone to Timbere for a few days.

"*My bracelets will find her,*" assured Tamara. Holding hands, Tamara instructed her bracelets to find Queen Astrid. In a moment, they were in Timbere, watching her sleep. They placed wards around the palace that would prevent any unauthorized visitors from entering.

"Do you think the wards are strong enough?" asked Tamara.

"What if I add an extra layer from my store of shadow magic?" asked Sean.

"That should do it—shadow magic against shadow magic," approved Tamara. *"That should get Scimitar's attention."*

"But if he reports it to the King, we may have put her in a more dangerous situation," warned Sean.

"What if you instruct the magic to remove the memory of any intruder?" suggested Tamara.

Sean chuckled, *"That's ingenious! What a good idea!"*

"Do you think we should stay until morning? I'd like to make sure the Queens are safe," asked Tamara.

"Morning isn't that far off," noted Sean. *"I'll tend to the shadow magic layer while you doze, if you like,"* offered Sean.

"I'm going to message Savea and Solange," proposed Tamara. *"I think it would be a good idea if they help the Queens learn how to operate their new powers. They were very helpful to me when my powers were activated."* Sean nodded and they both went to work.

When Sean had finished adding a shadow magic layer to the wards, he sat next to Tamara and put his arm around her. Suddenly, they were jolted from slipping into a light doze by the arrival of the Super Sisters.

Solange complimented Tamara on her idea of assisting the Queens in exploring their new powers. Savea mentioned that, when that project was completed, she intended to see Astrid safely to Seaside. *"The details you placed in your message concern me greatly,"* she added. *"The threats against Astrid and her kingdom are significant and I intend to stay until we deal with them."*

"That's a relief," sighed Tamara. *"Your generosity frees Sean and me to search for those ancient volumes."*

Chapter 8
Finding the Volumes

After bringing the Sisters up-to-date on what they had learned during the astral journey, Tamara held Sean's hand and instructed her bracelets to take them back to the cave in Brimstone.

She was surprised when they found themselves in what seemed to be Scimitar's personal kingdom. Populated entirely by artificial beings, this kingdom seemed to be devoted to granting Scimitar's every desire.

Scimitar was sprawled on a lava throne, and seemed to be talking to himself. "I served Lucas well and, what does he do? He threatens to make me one of his victims—as if he hadn't already done so to my real body. It's insulting! It's demeaning!

If only he would behave like he did in the old days—before I discovered those blasted books! I wish I could turn back time and destroy them!

Standing, he stepped down from the throne and began to pace back and forth. "I wonder....

"That's what I'll do! I'll find the books and eliminate

them!!! I don't need to deal with the Queen today; I gave her until the end of the week."

As he started to teleport, Tamara gave her bracelets an order to follow him. In a few minutes, they were back in the cave, shadowing Scimitar and silently proceeding deeper into the mountain. His progress took many twists and turns. Tamara was glad that they were on an astral journey; they wouldn't have to remember the details of their walk in order to return to the cave entrance.

Scimitar stopped when he reached what looked like a rockfall. Waving his hands, he moved the rocks away from a hidden recess. A pile of books rested on a shelf, glowing in a soft red light. Scimitar sent bolts of red lightning toward the books, but was knocked on his back by what seemed to be a force field. Muttering to himself, he tried a different spell, but had the same result.

Seeking shelter behind a stalagmite, Tamara and Sean watched a ghostly image of the King solidify next to Scimitar. "You traitor!" it hissed. "You are trying to betray me!" A black haze covered Scimitar and turned him into ash, which blew away farther into the cave. Tamara looked at Sean in horror and touched her travel crystal.

*   *   *   *   *

Back in her bedroom, Tamara trembled in Sean's arms.

He held her tightly and soothed her with soft words. *"That was horrible,"* she wept. *"I know he was an avatar, but he was a realistic one. It's clear that those books have to be destroyed, but I have no idea how to do it."*

"Nor do I," admitted Sean. *"But I need to report this act of shadow magic to Dana's Team. Will you be all right if I leave for a short time?"*

She nodded bravely, but after he left, she called for her mother. Terra appeared immediately and led her daughter to a nearby couch. Holding her hands, she asked Tamara what had happened. Tearfully, Tamara related all that had happened on the astral journey. Terra sent a calming spell into Tamara and the trembling stopped. She helped Tamara into bed and tucked the covers around her. Murmuring a sleep-enhancing spell, she silently left the room.

After reporting to the Watcher Council, Terra decided to join Sean and Dana's Team. Her sudden appearance startled them, but they were getting used to her comings and goings. Sean asked, *"Is Tamara still upset?"*

Terra responded that she was asleep. *"I'd like to hear your observations about what you witnessed, Sean,"* she said. *"The shadow magic within you may interpret things differently."*

"I watched with horror," he replied, *"but a small part of*

me appreciated the efficiency of the King's action."

"*And how did you feel after you added that layer of shadow magic to the wards protecting the palace in Timbere?*" she pressed.

"*Satisfied that my effort would succeed,*" he responded.

"*It sounds to me that shadow magic is totally without empathy or emotion,*" she concluded. "*We must keep that in mind as we continue this discussion.*"

"*That's a very astute observation, Terra,*" Jon added. "*I wonder how we could neutralize that goal-driven lack of morality.*"

"*Would it be possible to take an equal amount of clear magic and merge it with the shadow magic inside you, Sean?*" asked Dana.

"*That's an interesting thought,*" complimented Terra. "*I'll ask the Watcher Council if it's ever been done.*" And she vanished.

It wasn't long before she returned. She smiled as she reported that there was precedence for neutralizing shadow magic. "*I would have to help you,*" she offered. "*But the Head Watcher recommended that we wait. You may need the shadow magic when you have to confront King Lucas.*"

"*Did you learn anything about how we might defeat the considerable amount of shadow magic that King Lucas controls?"* asked Sean.

"No, I'm sorry," Terra replied. *"A challenge like that has never been done before. All I can suggest is that when the time is right, you and Tamara do it together. Remember what the Creator Being foretold: success would come through her."*

Sean and Jon looked at each other and frowned. At the present moment, they could not identify any path forward.

*   *   *   *   *

Meanwhile, Tamara was having a nightmare. She was standing at a precipice, watching Sean do battle with King Lucas. Bolts of shadow magic flew back and forth, but neither one seemed to be winning the encounter.

She called out to Sean, but he didn't hear her. She tried again and King Lucas turned toward her, sending a bolt of shadow magic in her direction. Fear clutched at her and she awakened, screaming. Mia rushed to her side. Terra suddenly appeared and joined them. She hugged her daughter and said, *"The time is almost upon us."*

Chapter 9
Teaching the Queens

Savea and Solange had been working with the Queens for days. Both women were quick learners and the Super Sisters from Marinea were satisfied with their progress. Queen Flora wanted to go with the Sisters to escort Queen Astrid home to Seaside. She had never visited that kingdom and was curious.

Teleporting to Seaside was done in the blink of an eye. When they entered the palace, they were greeted by King Lucas and a small army. Brandishing their weapons, they threatened the four women and demanded the sacrificial victims that they required.

Smiling, the women erected a defensive barrier and, at the same time, produced a shipping container that would carry the invaders back to Brimstone. The soldiers looked to the King for guidance. He shrugged and dismantled the container. Savea gestured to Astrid to send the intruders home. She waved her hands and a silver haze encircled them. In a moment, they were gone. "Well done," praised Savea.

"This is only the beginning," warned Astrid. "They will

be back."

"*King Lucas is now aware that you are not helpless,*" stressed Solange, switching to mental communication. "*He has to rethink his Game plan; it won't work anymore.*"

"*Don't worry, Astrid,*" counseled Flora, "*I won't leave you alone to fight him.*"

"*Nor will we,*" assured Savea and Solange together.

"*However, this will be the first encounter with shadow magic for all of us,*" reminded Solange. "*We need to plan and strategize.*"

*   *   *   *   *

The next morning, after a sumptuous breakfast of juice, crab cakes, eggs, toast, jelly and tea, the Super Sisters began to pepper Queen Astrid with questions. They were trying to get a sense of what the interactions between Astrid and King Lucas had been in the past. Clearly, he had used intimidation to break her spirit and create a climate of fear.

They were surprised when Terra suddenly appeared and asked to join them. "*I have intel from the Watcher Council to share,*" she explained. "*Dana's Team has already been briefed. You will need my help to do when I'm about to suggest. There is evidence that shadow magic can be neutralized with an equal amount of clear magic. When King Lucas arrives, which I believe will be shortly, I will grab one of his hands*" *while holding the hand of Flora, if she's willing."*

"Of course," Flora agreed, *"I'll do whatever is necessary."*

"With me as the intermediary, the amount of each type of magic should result in balance," Terra continued, *"producing a blended magic without immediate power. The power will return, but only after an extended period of time when the magical types become unique again.*

"I must stress that this is a 'band-aid' solution, but it should confuse the King and buy us some time."

"I think I hear visitors at the palace door," said Queen Astrid, standing. "Shall we greet them in the foyer?"

Linking arms, the four Super Children strode into the foyer. Holding Flora's hand, Terra moved forward and stood before King Lucas. "Good morning, Sire," she said, extending her hand. When he took it, he cringed and slumped to the floor.

"Welcome to Seaside, Sire," smiled Queen Astrid. "I have decided to refuse your request for sacrificial victims. You are free to return to your kingdom now." Waving her hand, she sent a silver haze toward the King and his men, and they disappeared.

"It worked!" crowed the four women. Terra asked Flora how she felt, who responded that she was a bit weakened, but she would recover soon.

Terra reminded the Queens that they should remain in each other's company until this entire duel with King Lucas had played itself out. *"That may take some time, so be prepared,"* she said.

"I must return to Marinea now and report our success to Dana's team. Just call my name if you need me and I will come. But before I go, I must retrieve Kalia, the new Ambassador from Marinea. She has been training with Talia on Timbere," she related.

"Before you go, Terra," Astrid interrupted, *"How should we behave if the King shows up and you are not here?"*

"I hope you have internalized how powerful you are," stressed Terra. *"One of you must serve as the channel and touch his hand, while holding the hand of the other who is willing to contribute good magic to the process temporarily.*

"Solange and Savea must return with me now. The time of the ultimate battle is nearing and we must prepare," warned Terra. Nodding, the Super Sisters touched her and all three vanished.

*   *   *   *   *

"Do you know what the 'ultimate battle' is?" asked Flora, wisely selecting mental communication.

"I think it will be the final showdown between good and evil magic, between clear and shadow magic," guessed Astrid.

"*Will we be part of the battle?*" wondered Flora.

"*Our lack of experience may preclude that,*" Astrid suggested. "*I guess we will have to wait and see.*"

Linking arms, they returned to the breakfast table to enjoy another cup of tea. As they were chatting, a staff member appeared to announce that the new Ambassador had arrived. The two Queens stood and enthusiastically welcomed her.

*　*　*　*　*

Tamara opened one eye and decided to snuggle deeper into her covers. Looking up at the skylight, she saw that it was definitely day and she reluctantly threw off the blankets. Sitting on the edge of her bed, she wondered when Sean had greeted the day.

As if in answer to her question, he entered the room and hurried to give her a 'good morning' hug.

"*Why did you let me sleep in?*" she asked.

"*Yesterday was a tough day for you,*" he explained, "*and Mia told me you had a bad nightmare. You needed some restorative sleep.*"

Tamara shuddered as memories of that nightmare began to surface. "*I don't think it was a dream,*" she judged. "*I think it was a vision of what is to come.*"

"*In that case,*" he prompted, "*I need to hear every detail that you remember. I know it will be painful, but your experience may contain valuable clues as to how we should prepare."*

Putting his arms around Tamara, he listened carefully to every word she spoke.

Chapter 10
Seeking a Path Forward

As soon as Tamara had dressed, she and Sean proceeded to the boat for breakfast. The rest of the Defense Team had already eaten, so Sean began the meeting, allowing Tamara to refuel her body.

Noticing that the Brothers and Terra were at the table, he shared his gratitude, and expressed the hope that they would consider themselves permanent members of the Team. The battle that was looming would require the skills of everyone.

Terra spoke next and related all that had happened in the kingdoms of Timbere and Seaside. Tamara summarized their astral journey and reported that both the real and artificial bodies of Scimitar had perished under the power of King Lucas. She pointed out that Scimitar's quest for global domination was actually an extension of the King's ambition.

There was an immediate sigh of relief, followed by a realization of the extent of the King's power.

Sean added that Lucas' power was derived from a stack of ancient volumes, containing the secrets of shadow magic. He stressed that eliminating those books was a top priority if they hoped to quell the King's ambition.

"*But how can we eliminate them?*" asked Sunan. "*You told us that Scimitar tried and was unsuccessful—and he was much more powerful than Sostor and I were, together!*"

"*I don't have any answers for you,*" admitted Sean. "*We will have to be both observant and patient. If an opportunity presents itself, we need to be ready to act.*"

"*Even though we have no idea what those actions might be?*" pressed Sostor.

"*Yes,*" affirmed Sean.

"*One avenue I rely on,*" suggested Tamara, "*are my bracelets. They come to my aid when I ask, whether consciously or unconsciously. But I'm reluctant to do so, since I'm never sure what direction they will pursue.*"

"*It is a risk,*" admitted Sean. "*However, it's good to know that they are capable of providing assistance.*"

"*Does anyone have thoughts or clues about what Lucas might try next?*" asked Savea. "*Several of his plans have been thwarted by the Queens, and I don't suppose that he was expecting that result. I'm unclear whether he will push forward in their direction, or come at us in revenge.*"

Jon broke in, "*I think we had better anticipate all possibilities that we can imagine, and prepare multi-faceted defenses. This is not going to be an easy struggle, nor is the outcome going to be one that we might wish.*"

"*I'm passing out some potential next steps that he might take,*" interrupted Sean. "*Each of you is assigned to a team that will consider the threat and propose one or more defenses that we could employ. We'll meet back here tomorrow as usual and discuss your ideas. Please keep in mind that time is not on our side.*"

*   *   *   *   *

The next morning, the Defense Team met for breakfast as usual, but there were only frowns at the table. Solange and Savea spoke first, "*We had advised the Queens to be together until further notice. We asked them to notify us of any movement from the King. Hearing nothing, we have decided to pay them another visit.*"

Jon and Dana summarized the thinking of their Team—which was essentially 'wait and see'. "*We need more intel before we can design a strategy that might work.*"

Sostor and Sunan just shook their heads. "*We have been so traumatized by Scimitar and his ability to control us. Thinking clearly is a big ask!*"

Terra and Trident were also without any ideas. "*We've ordered all the Ambassadors to be vigilant and alert us to any movement by King Lucas. So far, we have heard nothing.*"

"*That leaves Tamara and me,*" sighed Sean. "*I was*

hoping some ideas might have surfaced, but I see that I was too optimistic. Our only path forward seems to be using Tamara's bracelets. We have no way of predicting what direction that might take, however. Is anyone interested in joining us on an astral journey?"

"Of course I'll join you, Brother," proclaimed Jon. *"We're much stronger together."*

"And, since this seems to be a family affair," added Terra, *"I'll come along, too."*

Sunan looked at Sostor and nodded, *"While you are gone, we will work with Dana's Team to learn more about shadow magic."*

"Hopefully," Sean said, *"We will be back to meet with you tomorrow. Good luck, everyone."*

*   *   *   *   *

Terra and Jon met Sean and Tamara in their bedroom. The new large bed accommodated all four of them and they began to relax. Tamara asked her bracelets if those antique volumes could be destroyed or effectively contained—and the bracelets started to glow. Soaring into the sky, they headed away from daylight and toward the darkness.

Instead of landing near the caves of Brimstone, they found themselves in the undersea kingdom formerly inhabited by Scimitar. King Lucas was sprawled across the throne, talking to an avatar. "I rather like this kingdom he created for himself," Lucas commented. "It's much more comfortable than living in a cave. Have you relocated the magic volumes for me yet?"

"Yes, Sire," replied the avatar. "I did as you requested and put them in a secure location where no one will expect to find them."

"Excellent," praised Lucas. "And that location is?"

"Secure, Sire."

"WHERE IS IT?" demanded Lucas.

"I cannot tell you, Sire, or it wouldn't be secure."

Sean and Jon looked at each other, joined hands, and shot a black ray at the avatar—who disintegrated before their eyes. Lucas roared and looked around wildly, "Who is there? What have you done?" He began to cast spells randomly about, while screaming incoherently. Tamara touched her crystal and they were back in her bedroom.

"Well, I guess that's a temporary fix!" laughed Jon. *"The volumes are no longer an immediate threat."*

"True," replied Sean, *"But we have to keep them on our radar. That wasn't a permanent solution."*

Chapter 11
Pursuing Clues

Solange and Savea teleported to Seaside to check on the Queens. It was a warm reunion. Sitting around a table on a palace terrace with a marvelous view of the sea, they sipped on tea and enjoyed biscuits and jam. Kalia, the new Ambassador from Marinea joined them.

"*Has King Lucas contacted you in any way?*" asked Solange.

"*No,*" replied Queen Astrid, "*which is very strange. He was so intimidating and insistent on being provided with victims—and now, not a peep out of him.*"

"*Well, he may not understand what has happened to you,*" proposed Queen Flora. "*You are no longer afraid of him and his dominance is threatened.*"

"*But he is so powerful,*" argued Astrid. "*I can't imagine that he would just leave me alone. Something must have changed in his kingdom.*"

At that moment, Terra appeared and accepted a cup of tea from Astrid. "*I have come to let you know that some Watchers have been assigned to Seaside and also to the other* two kingdoms. *They will be observers only and will not introduce themselves. Also, Queen Tamara, Sean and his brother have just returned from Brimstone."*

"Why did they go to Brimstone?" asked Astrid.

"I was with them on the astral journey," explained Terra. *"Tamara asked her bracelets how to destroy or deactivate the ancient volumes and they took us not to the caves, but to the undersea kingdom previously occupied by Scimitar."* Continuing her report, Terra briefed them on the temporary fate of the volumes and the extreme reaction of King Lucas.

"Well, that would explain why King Lucas hasn't been bothering me," commented Astrid. *"He is probably unsure of what to do, now that those magical books are no longer available to him. He may be unable to increase his power through shadow magic, and sacrificial victims would be of no present use to him."*

"The question is," Savea wondered, *"how long will this inactivity last? You need to be very alert to even the slightest difference in his current or future behavior. Please contact us with any intel that you can share."* The Sisters disappeared.

Kalia stared at the space where they had been just a minute before. *"Do they come and go like that often?"* she asked.

"*They are very powerful Super Children and can teleport at will,*" said Queen Astrid. "*You will get used to it. Have you found a suitable location for the Embassy? Or would you like some assistance?*"

Kalia shook her head and accepted the offer of assistance. Queen Astrid invited her to have breakfast tomorrow morning and said she would arrange for a staff member to bring information on suitable buildings.

*   *   *   *   *

Meanwhile, back in Marinea, Dana was welcoming Trilllium, Sostor and Sunan to a meeting of his Team. "*We have been investigating shadow magic for some time now, and have been unable to reach any conclusions. Hopefully, you will bring fresh eyes to our endeavor.*"

Sostor asked, "*I've heard Jon mention that you have personal copies of ancient and arcane books and manuscripts. Is that correct?*"

"*Indeed,*" replied Dana. "*But we have been searching through them with little success.*"

"*May we try?*" inquired Sostor, with a glance at Sunan.

"*Certainly,*" answered Dana.

"*This spell is actually framed as a question,*" added Sunan. "*We will focus it on the books and pose the question of how to defeat or eliminate shadow magic*"

The Brothers joined hands and chanted while pointing toward the identified books and manuscripts. A white haze surrounded the materials as the Brothers intensified their chanting. Dana, Trillium and the Team watched with amazement as several books and manuscripts rose into the air and floated over to the table, opening to certain pages.

When the Brothers had finished chanting, they walked over to the table and began to examine the open pages. The rest of the Team joined them in their search. Time passed as the examination continued.

Suddenly, Dana and Sostor cried out together, *"I've found something!"* Sunan also proclaimed that he had discovered a clue.

Everyone clustered around them, peering over their shoulders. Dana spoke first, *"I'm looking at a spell that would change shadow magic into clear magic. It's intended to be cast when confronting a wielder of shadow magic—in this case, King Lucas."*

"That would be very useful," approved Sostor. *"What I've found could be done at the same time, freezing the wielder and preventing any pushback."*

"Mine is more far-ranging," added Sunan. *"It would sanitize a large area from anything past or present that was created with shadow magic. But there is no mention of whether*

it could be activated from the astral plane."

"*The safer path would be to engage the King on the reality plane,*" proposed Sostor. "*Even though the Sisters were able to vanquish that Prime Minister from the astral plane, he was carrying both forms of magic. We don't know what percentage was shadow, but that shard Terra found wasn't very large.*"

"*I agree,*" said Sunan. "*But I have to assume that the King has been accumulating shadow magic for some time. Queen Astrid has been pressured for sacrificial victims for what sounded like many months, if not years.*"

"*Is there any indication in what you have found that suggests what would happen to the King if we employ all three spells simultaneously?*" asked Trillium.

Both Sostor and Sunan shook their heads. Sostor spoke first, "*I wouldn't worry about it. He had been seriously abusing magic and doesn't deserve sympathy.*"

"*Plus, Sostor and I are coming from memories of personal abuse,*" added Sunan. "*It is increasingly clear that King Lucas was the driving force behind Scimitar and his efforts to control us.*"

The Brothers hugged and spent some time describing the trauma they had endured at the hands of Scimitar. Trillium added details from his experience as well. Dana and the Team were astonished at the severity of what the King and Scimitar had inflicted.

Dana thanked the Brothers for participating in the meeting, and helping so significantly with identifying a path forward. He welcomed Trillium as a new member of the Team and asked everyone to come to the breakfast meeting on the boat the following day. There would be much to share.

Chapter 12
Preparing for Battle

There were no frowns at breakfast the next day. There would be significant progress to report. First to arrive were Tamara and Sean. Soon after, the Brothers and Dana's Team, including Trillium, joined them. The Sisters and Terra completed the group.

"Now, let's eat and we'll get to the extremely important business of this meeting."

*   *   *   *   *

Tamara, Jon and Sean began the discussion by reporting on their astral journey. When they reached the part about King Lucas and his avatar, everyone was roaring with laughter. *"I guess we won't worry about Lucas learning any new Shadow Magic skills,"* observed Sostor.

"But it has to remain on the table," advised Sunan. *"Someone might find those volumes in the future and we'll have to deal with it."*

"It's clear that Lucas is power-hungry," observed Tamara. *"We don't know what else he might come up with. Savea, do you and Solange plan to return to Seaside for support"*?

Solange responded, *"Savea is going back in order to accurately map the volcanos and the sea. That side of Akura seems to be so volatile seismically. We need to be ready for what may occur. I plan to remain here, but I can get there in an instant if needed.*

"I should add that Kalia was also present when we were there. Queen Astrid will be helping her find appropriate locations for both the Embassy and her personal space."

The next speakers were Sostor, Trillium and Sunan. They presented what they had gleaned from their examination of the volumes. It became apparent that their inclusion in the work of Dana's Team was very beneficial. Sean had already appointed Trillium to the Team, but now he felt compelled to ask the Brothers if they would like to be formally added as well. The Brothers smiled at each other and enthusiastically agreed to be officially part of the Team.

Tamara congratulated everyone on a successful beginning to preparing for battle. *"Your efforts are significant,"* she praised, *"but keep in mind that this is only the introductory phase. Since we have no idea about when the conflict will actually start, we need to proceed with all possible speed.*

"When King Lucas decides to move aggressively, we don't know whether it will be on his side of the planet or ours.

We must be prepared for both possibilities. Think about it for the rest of today and bring your thoughts and ideas to tomorrow's breakfast meeting."

*   *   *   *   *

Meanwhile, in Seaside, Kalia was having breakfast with Queen Astrid. Kalia had been the grateful recipient of magic glasses from Solange and intended to wear them at all times. When she looked up, a young woman was walking toward them with a pile of papers. Kalia was pleased that she seemed to be real.

"Ah, I see that Margo has arrived," announced Astrid, switching to mental communication. "S*he will be your guide today as you look at appropriate properties. I think the two of you will have a good time together!*"

Kalia thanked the Queen sincerely and followed Margo into a small office nearby to look at the materials. She had already decided that she preferred to have her personal residence nearby, but not in the same building as the Embassy. With that preference in mind, she separated the documents into two piles and chose several properties from each to view today.

The two women agreed to look at potential Embassy locations first. Margo looked at Kalia's favorites and placed them in ranked order according to desirability and practicality. The very first building that they visited was close to the palace.

As soon as Kalia entered, she walked through it from a security point of view and was totally satisfied. She then asked Margo for her opinion.

Margo pointed out the benefits of the building, stressing that the first floor could be used for receptions and small meetings; the second floor was ideally arranged already for staff offices. Kalia agreed and asked Margo to make the necessary arrangements.

Once that decision had been made, Kalia was ready to look for a place to live. Margo smiled and took a paper from the top of the residence pile and handed it to Kalia, who noted that it was right on the shore and only a block from the Embassy choice. She could hardly wait to see it!

*   *   *   *   *

Queen Astrid was waiting for Queen Flora to join her for lunch. She had spent the morning signing official documents and was definitely ready for a relaxing time with her new Sister. As Flora entered the terrace, she waved to Astrid and smiled. As they chatted over lunch, Flora invited Astrid to return with her to Timbere. There were some duties that needed attention, and she was very conscious of the need to remain together.

"*That sounds lovely,*" approved Astrid. "*I would enjoy that break away from my office. Shall we leave right after dessert?*"

Hearing a commotion at the palace front door, Flora grabbed her Sister's hand and said, "*I think right now would be best.*" And they vanished.

*   *   *   *   *

Arriving instantly in her palace in Timbere, Flora sent a mental message to Savea and hurried inside. She was grateful that the wards Tamara had placed around the palace were still active. Savea and Solange were waiting for them. "*You have excellent instincts,*" praised Savea. "*King Lucas and a small force were at your doorstep. This may be the first salvo of his intended invasion.*"

"*But my kingdom!*" cried Astrid. "*I can't allow him to take it without a fight!*"

"*Don't worry, my dear,*" soothed Solange. "*We won't let that happen. I've alerted Tamara. She and Sean will join us in a moment.*"

As she predicted, Tamara, Jon and Sean arrived and walked toward them. "*Jon,*" said Solange, "*I'm so delighted to see you!*"

Sean informed them, "*I've asked Tamara to make a policy that when there is a threat, Super Children should face it together because they are stronger that way.*"

71

     "That's an excellent suggestion, Sean," affirmed Savea. *"Shall we see what's going on in Seaside?"*

Chapter 13
The Battle Begins

Tamara and the six Super Children teleported into the Seaside palace, discovering it surrounded by armed avatars and King Lucas lounging on Astrid's throne. As they walked toward the throne, King Lucas stood and sneered at them, "Well, who do we have here? I wondered where you were, Queen Astrid. Who are your friends?"

"What are you doing here, King Lucas?" asked Astrid. "What gives you the right to sit on my throne?"

"I do whatever I please, as you well know," boasted King Lucas. "I've come for the sacrificial victims you owe me. Your friends can be part of that package."

"I told you when you were here before that I no longer will accede to your demands," Astrid retorted.

"So you did," admitted King Lucas. "Therefore, your kingdom is forfeit and you will be added to the package." Stepping down from the throne, he aimed a black haze at Astrid, who erected a defensive barrier. Flora grabbed her hand and the two queens turned the haze back toward Lucas.

He screamed and dissolved into a puddle on the floor.

"*Clearly, that was an avatar*," observed Jon. "*Sean, let's clean up the garbage outside.*"

The two men left the room and the Queens hugged in relief. "Would anyone like some refreshment?" asked Astrid in a quavering voice.

Everyone nodded and walked out to the terrace. Staff members hastened to bring snacks and drinks to their guests.

Tamara commented, "*While that drama was unfolding, I put on my glasses and could not tell that Lucas was not real. That is very disturbing.*"

Sean returned with Jon and joined the others. They had heard Tamara's statement and were also concerned. Jon offered a possible solution, "*When Trina and I were looking for possible Embassy properties, she preferred a three-story building. I made the search easier by casting a spell that made all buildings fitting that description take on a golden glow. I'd like to try that spell on your glasses, Tamara, asking that all avatars appear with a golden glow.*"

Tamara smiled, "*That would be wonderful, Jon. I hope it works.*" Jon proceeded with the spell; now they would have to wait until their paths crossed with an avatar to be sure.

Savea raised her glass to toast the two Queens, "*I am so proud of you both. You handled that situation beautifully. How are you feeling?*"

"*Unsettled,*" admitted Astrid.

"*Angry,*" testified Flora.

"*Both reactions are understandable,*" soothed Solange. "*We now have to figure out where to go from here. Sean, we need advice from a military expert.*"

Sean thought for a moment, and then advised, "*Both Queens need to rule their kingdoms, but I recommend that you continue to stay together and split your time between the two kingdoms. Your behavior today is clear evidence that you can effectively work as a team, even in stressful situations.*"

The two Queens smiled at each other and held hands, pleased at receiving such a kind compliment. When the refreshments had been consumed, the visitors teleported home, leaving the Queens peacefully looking out to sea.

*   *   *   *   *

Back in Marinea, Tamara sat in Sean's office and watched the vid screens. She asked Sean if he had been able to create enough birds to monitor the new kingdoms as well as the known. Hearing a positive reply, she sighed and began to relax. "Oh no!" cried Sean, as he rushed to her side. Her bracelets were glowing brightly and the newlyweds were off on another unanticipated astral journey.

*   *   *   *   *

They found themselves once more in the kingdom of

Brimstone. King Lucas was pacing back and forth, yelling and punching the cave walls with fury. "They destroyed my best personal avatar!" he screamed. "How dare they!"

Moving his hands as if he were sculpting a human figure, a new personal avatar began to take shape. Muttering to himself, he complained, "If I have to continue replacing myself, I'll use up my shadow magic. That would be unacceptable. I need to have a foolproof plan that will let me accomplish my goals without sacrificing any more shadow magic."

Striding more deeply into the cave, he eventually reached an area that was glowing red. Sean and Tamara followed him quietly, careful to not alert him to their presence. They watched him put his hands into a pile of glowing red lava. The red glow crawled up his arms and eventually encompassed his entire body. Apparently fortified once more, he returned to where his new personal avatar waited. Clasping the avatar by the shoulders, Lucas transmitted a red glow into the avatar. "There!" he crowed. "No one will be able to destroy YOU!" He whispered instructions to the avatar and sent him on a mission. "Those Queens will rue the day they decided to reject my orders!"

Sean and Tamara looked at each other with horror. Tamara touched her travel crystal and they were back in Sean's office.

"*We must return to Seaside immediately, but on the reality plane,*" stressed Tamara. "*I'll notify the others.*"

Sean nodded and said, "*Round Two of the battle is about to begin.*"

About the Author

After doing academic writing during my 20 years as Professor at the University of Wisconsin-Madison, I retired to Hawai'i in 1999. A decade later, I began being aware of an interesting fantasy story line in my mind and began writing it soon after. It was an occasional hobby for another decade and then the book became impatient with me and began to seriously nudge me. Since I began "listening" to the book, the writing has been a fun and all-encompassing part of my life.

I have completed 12 books in my Crystal Saga Series 1 and and so far, 2 books in Crystal Saga Series 2. More to come.

Crystal Saga Series 1 by
D. E. Weingand

Book 1 — Tamara's Crystals

Book 2 — Genesis Explored

Book 3 — Masquerade

Book 4 — Discoveries

Book 5 — Gamesmanship

Book 6 — Beginnings

Book 7 — Looking Forward . . . and Backward

Book 8 — Making Progress

Book 9 — Searching for Truth

Book 10 — The Truth is Out There

Book 11 — Finding Truth

Book 12 — Loose Ends

 *Scan the QR Code with Your Cell Phone to Order Books. Or go to LuLu.com, Amazon.com, Barnsandnoble.com and many other outlets.*

Crystal Saga Series 2 by
D. E. Weingand

Book 1 — Exploration

Book 2 — More Mysteries

Coming Soon

Book 3 — Escalation

Book 4 — To be announced